D15296893

FORMING HABITS

Short Stories by Mary Martin Riser

With best wishes,

Mary Martin Riser

Swamp Fox Press, LLC
Gulf Breeze, Florida

First Edition

Swamp Fox Press, LLC
P.O. Box 411
Gulf Breeze, Florida 32562-0411
SAN 253-5998

p. cm.
LCCN 00-111687
ISBN 0-9706473-1-X

1. Women—Southern States—Conduct of life—Fiction.
I. Title.

PS3568.I653F67 2001   813'.6
                               QBI01-902115

Other than the memoir of Miss Antigone Papageorge, any resemblance
to actual events or persons, living or dead, is entirely coincidental and
not the intent of the author.

COVER PHOTO BY MARY MARTIN RISER

FOR MY SONS,
MARSHALL AND WALTON

ACKNOWLEDGEMENTS

I WOULD LIKE TO THANK JIM WHITE FOR SHOWING, NOT TELLING ME HOW TO WRITE, SUSAN TUCKER FOR BEING AN INSPIRATION, REBECCA REEVES FOR HER ENCOURAGEMENT, AND KIM BANCROFT WOOD FOR HER KNOWLEDGE OF THE ENGLISH LANGUAGE. ALSO, SPECIAL APPRECIATION GOES TO SWAMP FOX PRESS.

CONTENTS

PREFACE

As Robert Frost reminds us in "The Road Not Taken", our lives are defined by the choices we make. Although women have progressed professionally, some have difficulty, even inability, making decisions concerning home, family, friends, and lovers. These stories are about the choices the women characters make or, in the case of "Miss Antigone Papageorge" or Bartie in "Ladies on Their Birthdays", how they handle those made for them. The characters in "Forming Habits" and "Flag-Waving Proud" have made positive and enriching decisions. Others, like the preacher's wife in "Dixie Whistles" and Ellen, until she takes control of her life at the end of "Locations", have surrendered their options and lead unfulfilled lives. Bessie, in "Bessie's Story", demonstrates strength not in her choices, but in her reactions to events. Amelia of "Riding the Waves" and Suzanne in "Living Well" have chosen death because they are unable to discern alternative paths.

These stories are reflections of lives and have been written from within, based on places I have been and events that have taken place, sometimes only in my mind. I respect the fictional female characters and hope to get into their skin as they have gotten under mine and to show life from the points of view of different women.

WOMAN'S WORK

Bessie brushed my hair and it hurt,

She told me all peoples have tangles in their hair.

Sadie taught me manners and washed my mouth out with soap

When I said nigger or lied.

She made me lemon pie when I was lonely.

Alma showed me how to wash myself

And explained ghosts.

Yvonne was my confidante and kept my secrets like her own.

I've known black angels,

They have guided me through life.

When all is over,

I pray a black angel will cradle me to death.

MMR
June 25, 1994

BESSIE'S STORY

Bessie and her sister, Sadie, came to Johnson when they were just girls. There wasn't any work in Camden and their mama said for them to go south and talk to Malcolm Smith, my grandfather. She said he came from back home and was bound to hire them. So, sixteen-year-old Bessie and seventeen-year-old Sadie walked all the way here. They set out before day and got to our place about the time the sun was setting in the cornfield. They walked up the brick driveway, both of them barefooted – some of the old pavers were broken up and crumbling in places – so they had to watch their steps. The drive curved in front of the biggest house they'd ever seen. They stood and looked at each other when they got to it. Four white columns across the wide porch were ten feet tall, and they were feeling mighty short. Sadie grabbed Bessie's hand when she started up the brick steps and whispered they should go to the back.

They stepped onto the grass and walked past a rose garden laid out around a marble statue of a lady with a stream of water pouring out her overturned urn. There were pink, red, and yellow roses, some budding and some fully blown. It reminded them of their mama 'cause she loved roses more than anything. They had a Lady Banks climbing over their porch at home. Those flowers made them a little homesick at the time, but Bessie says she has taken comfort in them since and likes to see them out the kitchen window when she washes dishes. They were met at the back screen door by my great-aunt, Miss Margaret. She is Grandmother's spinster sister who used to teach sixth grade. She welcomed them like they were company, sat them down at a pine table in the kitchen, and got each a tall glass of ice water before going to get Grandmother. Bessie looked over the table at a picture of a crooked man ambling up a winding path, gripping a bent walking stick in his hand. She wondered where he was going and thought she might know how he felt. An old colored lady with white hair pulled back in a bun was stirring vegetable soup at the stove. She told them her name was Molly and that she lived in the Quarters under the hill near the lumber mill.

Grandmother came in. She was a little woman with dark, wavy hair held back by clips. Bessie said she reminded her of the duchess who stole the king of England. It had been in all the papers and some thought it romantic, but Bessie said it was disgusting for a divorcee hussy to go over there and mess in them folks' business like it was her

2

own. Grandmother asked them a couple of questions about their trip. She said Malcolm's sister-in-law had written her about Bessie and Sadie, and she'd been expecting them. She told Molly to fix them some soup and sandwiches and said Molly would let them stay at her house 'til they could get settled. Bessie told me later that Grandmother was nice and didn't act like a duchess at all.

In no time, they were fixed up in a light green, wooden house with two bedrooms and an inside bathroom. They could walk back and forth from the big house to theirs on the clay road that led to everything on the farm. Bessie said they'd never seen such dirt before, in Camden it was chocolate brown. Here the earth is solid red.

There were seven houses for coloreds, and theirs was next door to Dave and Lucille's. They raised turkeys and chickens and had six children, all sent to them by relatives. Dave had stabbed his first wife with a butcher knife, caught her in bed with another man. Killed him, too. When Malcolm got the farm from the state, Dave and Aaron were working on it. They were trustees. Dave said Malcolm told the warden if he was to buy the place, he'd need somebody familiar with it to stay. Dave was a gentle man who wouldn't harm anybody unless his passions were riled. Aaron, I don't know about. He was Malcolm's driver and lived in the set of rooms attached to the machine

3

shed. I wasn't allowed to visit him, but my brother snuck there and drank sugar-water with him. It was a drink they had in prison. Aaron was a rounder and never took a wife though we heard he had a bunch of children scattered around Pensacola. I hadn't met anybody who was really from Florida, but he said he was. Bessie said he was always bragging about what a cat he was down there. He flattered up to her and Sadie, but they didn't pay him any attention. Once, when Malcolm was gone to Washington, he offered to ride them through the Quarters in the Cadillac. Aaron took the car, and the law found him in Pensacola, in some juke joint, liquored up. That was the only time I ever saw Malcolm lose his temper. He told Aaron he better head on to Florida, said he was just messing up the fine state of Alabama.

Sadie met one of Molly's nephews while they were staying at her place, and before I knew what was what, she up and married P.J. Then there were three of them in the one house. Trim, Bessie's old beau from home, came into town proclaiming he was lovesick for her, and she, although she said she should have known better, believed him and they were married, too. Their house was small for so many grown folks, and Grandmother said there might be trouble if two couples stayed together, so she got Bessie another place. It had been Rufus and Little Baby's before

4

she ran off with another man. Rufus left looking for her. I think he would have been happier if he'd tried to find someone closer to his size. Little Baby, a mulatto from Monroe County, was so big that about all she could do was sit on the porch shelling peas or butterbeans. Bessie said she stopped by to visit a couple of times, but Little Baby wanted her to straighten up the house and mop the floors. Said she was too tired to do it. I think she was just too fat. I was surprised a man took up with her, but Bessie smiled and said men love big women. She's on the stout side herself.

Back home Bessie's job had been keeping her mama's house clean, so she was hired as housekeeper and Sadie as cook although Bessie made most of the desserts. Grandmother taught home economics in Briscoe City before Malcolm went there in his chauffeured car and swept her off her feet. She took Bessie and Sadie on as pupils. The food was pretty basic unless Grandmother was having a luncheon or bridge party. There were plenty of those. Grandmother and Aunt Margaret were both champion players and they loved cards. Bessie set up the living room with foldout tables covered in linen tablecloths of all colors and put out ashtrays. Sadie kept the ladies in hors d'oeuvres all day. They fretted about watching their figures but sure gobbled up the petit fours and ice cream balls Bessie rolled in shaved chocolate, coconut, and crushed pecans. Sadie made the ice cream on the back porch every Saturday morning. As soon as she got up, Grandmother drove to the ice plant and the IGA for ice, rock salt, and a bag of sugar. Bessie made custard from Grandmother's mother's recipe: ten eggs fresh from Dave's henhouse, two cups of sugar, and ten cups of milk from the cow, Daisy, who stayed in the lot next to the horse barn. Aunt Margaret would eat half of it if she could get away with it, but Grandmother made me keep an eye on her. She didn't eat desserts and didn't want a fat sister.

P.J. and Sadie started their family before Bessie and Trim. They had Janie and W.T. before Bessie's twins were born. Suzie and Suzie-Ann were like one person from the beginning. When one took a bite of food, the other chewed. I couldn't tell them apart; nobody but Bessie could, and I think they were more alike inside than out. They never needed anybody but themselves. Trim, Jr. came next. He was the spitting image of his father, and Bessie says that's why he always courted trouble. The baby was Meridian. I liked her name, thought it just sat there and glowed, full of pride. We were best friends from the start. Bessie said we were like rice and gravy, nothing could split us up.

Malcolm went to Mississippi once a month on business. Once he brought back a little brown clay jar that had Weidmann's Restaurant scratched on the side. He said it was the finest restaurant in the south. Said their pies were as good as Bessie's. That made her want to go and see them for herself. Grandmother got the recipe for their bourbon pie, and I have to admit, it was tasty. But I am partial to lemon, and people in Johnson say Bessie makes the best. She cooked one every Friday night, and Meridian walked over after supper and ate it with me.

I think Meridian meant more to Bessie than her other children. Sadie said she favored her too much. She said we shouldn't have been surprised at what happened. The Lord doesn't want you to get too attached to anything down here, but that's what Bessie did. She didn't love anything more than Meridian. She was a skinny little thing, a sack of sticks. She didn't eat much except sweets She loved dewberry cobbler, and when the season came in and the berries were ripening on the vines, nothing could hold her back. She and I stayed after Bessie to let us go picking. We'd return with ankles bloody from briar bites and fingernails stained deep blue, and it didn't matter if our pails were just half full, we were proud of our haul. We'd eat some of the treasures, but saved most for Bessie to cook 'specially for us. At night, she made cobbler at home with

Meridian standing on a chair by her side, mixing flour, sugar, and soda into the melted butter. She poured the sugared berries on top of the mixture, and when the cobbler came out of the oven, Meridian was surprised every time that the golden crust had risen and hidden the fruit.

Grandmother paid anybody on the farm for full baskets, and Bessie's twins and Sadie's girls sold all they could get. Sadie took the bought berries in their discolored containers to the basement and tied up bags of cheesecloth and hung them from the wooden beams above the trestle table in the middle of the room. Thick, dark liquid oozed and dripped from those swollen bags like milk from reluctant cows. When the sacks hung purple and dry, Sadie took the juice upstairs to the kitchen and boiled it with sugar, stirring with a long-handled metal spoon until it thickened and clung to the side. Bessie washed and sterilized mason jars so Sadie could ladle in the jelly, and she melted Gulfwax blocks to seal the boiling liquid. Then, they took the hot jars back to the basement, set them on plank shelves in the jelly cupboard, and latched the brass screened doors. Sadie said the bottles had to rest at least a month before they could be opened.

It was one of those clear, cloudless days in May when the wind, with just a hint of summer in it, races across the grass in gusts so small and frail it seems like ghosts playing on the lawn. Sadie's kids and Bessie's older children were at school, and Grandmother was hosting a luncheon to plan a fundraiser for the hospital auxiliary. The members were putting together a cookbook, and Aunt Margaret had talked Grandmother into including recipes from Bessie and Sadie. Molly, who had started working at Aunt Sally's house in town, was to be included, too. Sadie was torn between her secret remoulade sauce or gumbo; Bessie was going with lemon pie. Bessie was helping Sadie serve the lime congealed salad when Meridian and I appeared at the backdoor and asked to go pick berries. Grandmother had told me she wanted us out of the house when she had company. Bessie gave us two, old, metal pots and told us to watch out for snakespit. Any briars that had foam on them meant a snake was around for sure. She said they like dewberries as much as little girls did.

When the ladies finished lunch, Sadie served strawberry shortcake on her big, ice water biscuits, and Bessie stood at the sink washing dishes. Out the window the rosebushes were gently bobbing under the weight of huge blossoms. Creamy, yellow butterflies were dancing circles in the air and kissing petals soft as their wings. Bessie said she heard the crunch of tires on the driveway before she saw the old Plymouth pull around to the back and park in the deep shade of the oak tree that cooled the screen porch. A short, stocky man wearing a rumpled and faded gray shirt stuck to his chest with sweat got out of the car and walked slowly to the passenger's side and opened the door. I slid off the seat and moved in measured steps to the outside of the vehicle. The stranger stared at the car's backdoor before he touched the handle and opened it. He reached in and lifted a limp bundle as if it were the heaviest object in the world. He was walking toward the house like he was wading through mud, I at his side, when Bessie realized he was carrying her baby girl. She ran from the kitchen, a scream lodged in her throat. She was unable to make a sound although her head was exploding. She crashed through the screen door, hearing it bang against the wall of the house. Without looking at the face of the man, she tore her child from his arms and started down the path that led to her house. She passed the swing set where her little girl and I had hung like monkeys from the cold bars that had rubbed blisters on our palms. She passed the horses we had begged to ride. They grazed in the fresh green pasture, sunshine warming their backs, the delicate flavor of spring grass in their mouths. She walked straight ahead like she had a mission, as if her calm, reassuring pace and steady gaze could bring back her baby. She carried her, her girl light as a sparrow, up their wooden steps which were sprinkled with red dust to ward off evil, across the planked floor where the clay pots sat, filled with seedlings sprouting the promise of summer, and into the cool, dark house. The twins and Trim, Jr. slept in the bedroom off the main room where the family spent evenings in front of the wood burning stove. Trim had left a year earlier saying he didn't want to be tied down, so Meridian had been sharing Bessie's room at the back of the house.

Bessie lay Meridian's empty body across the quilt her mama had made and sent at Christmas. She took the white socks, dyed purple from berry juice, off her bony ankles. She removed her pink shorts, striped shirt, and ruffled panties, folded and placed them in a drawer from which she took the dress Meridian had worn to Easter service six weeks earlier. She dressed her with the same deliberation she had seen Meridian use when she played with her doll. With one arm, Bessie lifted her limp body and held her back, and with the other, pulled the dress over her head and across her shoulders. When she completed clothing Meridian, she brought all the pillows and propped her head against them. In her organdy dress, Meridian looked like she was floating on a pale, peach cloud in a patchwork sea.

Bessie lay down beside her and stared at the ceiling, counting the boards running its length. She wanted to cry

11

but was unable. Sometimes grief comes suddenly and is so unexpected that your heart will not respond for fear of making things worse. Thoughts did not enter her mind. She was without connection to anything she had known or could imagine.

Sadie caught the children as they spilled out of the school bus and took them to her house. She must have known to leave her sister alone with her grief.

Late in the afternoon, as the day was closing in deep reds and oranges – the sun puts on a violent show in late May – Grandmother and I walked to Bessie's house, climbed the steps, leaned in, and knocked on the door she had left ajar. I thought she wasn't coming because she took so long, but finally Bessie appeared and came onto the porch. The two grown-ups sat without moving in weathered, old rockers, and I leaned against the porch rail. Grandmother asked me to tell Bessie the story.

We had picked all the berries we could find on the south side of the new four-lane that bordered the farm. Although we knew better, there weren't many cars passing by, and we imagined acres of ripe fruit on the bright green hillside across the highway. We made a pact to go together, holding hands like we'd been taught when crossing a street. We each picked up our pot by its black handle and ran as fast as possible over the first two lanes. Stopping in the median to catch our breath, we giggled with excitement at doing something we knew was wrong and made a promise never to tell anybody about our adventure. We clutched each other's sweaty palm and started across the first lane of two designed for traffic heading south. Meridian's pot slipped and hit the hot, black asphalt with a whack. She jerked her hand away from mine and reached down to pick it up. Some of the berries had fallen out and were rolling across the lane. Meridian was moving from one to another, bending over and scooping them up and back into the pot as I ran to the soft, grassy side of the road, yelling for her to hurry. Neither of us heard the whirring of the red Thunderbird as it raced down the highway. The car hit Meridian's body with a loud, clapping sound, tossed it over the hood, and pitched it high in the air. She landed in the weeds beside the pavement with a dull thud as the car sped down the road. I felt like my feet were glued to the ground as I tried to run toward her. I sat on the ground beside Meridian, cradled her head in my lap, and brushed dirt from her face and hair.

A salesman in a green Plymouth spotted us beside the highway. He was late for a meeting his boss was making him attend in Monroeville. He said he wouldn't have seen us if he had been going faster, but he was nervous about the presentation he was to give and hoping to miss the entire thing. He pulled his car to the shoulder and backed up. He got out and stood in front of us. I looked up and, without a word, he leaned down and took Meridian from me. I followed him to his car and watched him lay her still warm body on the hot, vinyl backseat. Without being asked, I climbed into the front, sat on the seat beside him and, speaking in a whisper, directed him the short distance to our house.

An owl in a dead oak tree across the pasture hooted for its mate. I heard Grandmother crying into her handkerchief, but no sound came from Bessie. I was afraid to look at her, so I let my eyes rest on the rough, cedar fence that kept cows out of her clean, swept yard. A morning glory vine was wrapped around the hand cut pickets, its flowers closed for the night. I wondered if there would be fresh blossoms in the morning.

MISS ANTIGONE PAPAGEORGE

In the summer of 1997, my friend, William Scourtes, asked me to interview his godmother, Miss Antigone Papageorge. William wanted recollections of the Malbis experience recorded for posterity's sake. I began visiting Miss Papageorge for an hour each afternoon, and she was generous enough to dictate her story, from memory, to me. She died the following winter. Today, only two of the original Malbis colony of residents remain on the plantation, Miss Bessie Pappas and Miss Lula Papa.

I would not like too much of this to be known. I was adopted from an orphanage in Pensacola and came to Malbis when I was four years old, almost an infant. I am eighty-four now. Living at Malbis has not just changed my life, it is all of my life. I want to see it as far as I can, and I am listening, and I am hoping a lot of nice things will be done for the time being to come. You know we can't be here forever, there's a limit to everything. I'm glad I grew up and lived here, every step has been beautiful. There have been good times and bad times, sad times and laughter.

Here is a picture of Grandma and Grandpa Papageorge. She wears a copy of a dress Queen Victoria wore in England. He has the style of the czar of Russia.

They were in government in Greece. Beside them is William, their son, and Photini, their daughter, my beloved, adopted mother. Her hair was dark and long down her back. It made a light around her.

William and Photini came here when Mr. Malbis did, 1906. Mr. Malbis was born in a small, mountain town in Greece, across from a monastery. He went to the monastery, after his parents died, to study his letters. That's the way people got an education back in those days. He stayed to be a priest. The monks were given a lot of things from the people. Rich people would leave their riches to have the monks pray for them after they died. Mr. Malbis got huge tips for praying. He was a hard worker, and when he left the monastery, he acquired property in a neighboring town and started olive oil manufacturing. When he traveled through the country on his way to Athens, he met people like the Papageorges, who had a big cherry orchard, and talked to them of his plans. They, like other people, were captivated by his dreams and supported his endeavors to go to the United States. He had the Malbis idea all along.

After Mr. Malbis and Uncle William got to Chicago in 1904, they secured funds to go around and look for land. They traveled down the west coast on a train, but didn't find what they were looking for until they got to Alabama in 1906. When they were shown the hundred and twenty acres that would become Malbis, Mr. Malbis, filled with emotion, said to William, "Stop! Don't go any farther. Here is the place we shall build. There is no doubt in my mind this is where our plans and goals will come true." The agreement was made to pay five dollars an acre, in installments, and Malbis was chartered in 1910.

Then everybody came down from Chicago – Mr. Galentas, Tom Matthews, and Uncle John. Uncle John was a self-disciplined person who noticed things in people, like when they were sick. There was no traffic here and no real road so it took hours to bring a doctor from Fairhope. But, Uncle John, like a medicine man, could do things to cure you. He had been a student to become a doctor, and he had been through, I don't know how many, classes. He could do the practical things too. For us children, he got up every morning and made a pot of hot milk and baked sweet potatoes. He would mash the sweet potatoes in our cups or bowls and we would pour in the hot milk. If you weren't able to have that, you would have milk toast. He would toast the bread on both sides real hard, put it in a dish, and pour hot milk with sugar over it. We wanted to be sick quite often. But, if you were really sick, they would put hot water in an old, old bathtub and put a long, thick towel down for the patient to lie there. They would place cold cloths on your head so you wouldn't die. The water was boiling hot and it had to be done in the kitchen. I hated that. I've had only one of those.

Uncle John was a wonderful person. He came from Bosphorus, in Turkey, and he stayed here fifty years. Everybody spoke Greek all the time, but since he spoke Turkish, they used "dog Latin" with him. Uncle John would say, "I don't understand. You talking behind my back." He had the most knowledge in the agricultural business and was able to give much to many things. He called Mr. Malbis, "My Captain, My Captain. My Captain, where are you?" On Saturday afternoons, the menfolk had time off and would sleep as late as they wanted. If there was a problem, Mr. Malbis, whose room was downstairs, would stand at the foot of the stairs and yell up to Uncle John whose room was at the top, "Yanni?"

"Yes, sir, My Captain?"

"Tomorrow it is going to rain. What are we going to do? We have to dig."

"I'll get everybody on the farm to work as much as we can today." Uncle John would take care of it.

In those days, we had chickens and cows. You mix sunflowers with corn and something that looks like wheat, but isn't really wheat down here, to make feed for the cattle. We also brought feed from a man in Loxley. At the time we had many colored people working here. Uzzie was a tall colored man. His family had so many children when he was born they had run out of names. They said, "You Z." I remember Washington, too. He was out in a storm, picking up manure with a rake. It had a wooden handle, but lightning went right through him. Mr. Malbis was depressed for a long time because an employee was killed.

Before farming, timber was our first industry. The original sawmill was built on a cliff but kept washing away. They kept fixing the roads but had to move it closer.

Then there was the turpentine. They would put yokes on the steer and oxen – we didn't have horses here – and make them walk through the pine trees. The colored people would take rosin off the trees by scraping them. We had thousands of pounds of it. Other men would come behind with the yoked oxen and fill square cans weighing one hundred pounds and put them on the animals, three to a unit. Then, little by little – you know what the pace of these animals is – they would pull the heavy wagons, with no rubber on the tires, to the pit. It was like a burning kettle, flat and thick, and they would let it boil. Then, bit by bit, the men would skim it off, throw the dirt out of the scrapings, and take the rosin to our little grocery store. There they made a round place (the top was as big as a TV), and they'd skim it and pour it into fifty pound cans that would eventually be sealed after the rosin rose. It had to be done just right, scraped in the spring and finished before cold weather returned.

Hercules Guletsos, a very short man, ran the grocery store. All the colored people used to come in after the turpentine was distilled. They'd have chips that represented pay. He would keep a record of what they got and how much they took on credit. The poor things had been worked all week, for just two dollars. A can of salmon was a dollar. What are they going to eat the rest of the week? Mr. Malbis said that was not fair and for them to have some food at the house.

Now, they needed rosin to clear the wines. In Greece, it is gotten from other sources, but we had to save it in cans. We sent some to the Papadeases and the Mallars in Chicago. They would see that the Greek people making wine illegally – it was the time of Prohibition – got it up there.

They made their own wine. You know you can make rum from sugarcane; they made wine from it. Uncle George Pappas came, and he knew all about vineyards. They kept a keg with spirits in it, like retsina, and another with wine. They used grapes from foreign lands like Venezuela, not Alabama muscadines. That was when wine was outlawed, also beer.

We had a house in Mobile and they were making beer. It was against the law, but there's not a Greek in the world who wouldn't have something to drink, you know. They had brewed the beer and put it in the little closet under the stairs in the middle of the hall. Tom Matthews, one of the oldtimers, had his bedroom right off the hall. He went to sleep, and the beer started fermenting and brewing. Then, it just blew from the heat and everything. They'd put the tops on too soon. When Tom Matthews heard all the noise, he thought they were having trouble with the Ku Klux Klan – of course, you know they were against all foreigners. He jumped up and ran into the hall, yelling, "All right, boys; all right, boys…" He was hollering upstairs to Mr. Angelo and Mr. George and all of them. He never lived that down. They called him a scaredy-cat from then on.

I took my name from my beloved adopted mother's middle initial. I took my last name from her, also. Miss Photini Papageorge was a young, brave woman, but she didn't live long. In 1918, there was a terrible flu, and she went to Chicago to take care of her aunt. She had been here, helping sick people and teaching everybody, trying to do everything, when she went to Chicago and caught the influenza and died. She had told her father when she left Greece with her brother and Mr. Malbis, "We are going over there, and we don't know what the customs are going to be." The funeral was held here in the house, and all the people called her an angel. Her parents came. They fell over the casket and cried and cried. Naturally, I was too young to know it was a fatal thing.

Mrs. Mallars was devastated when my adopted mother died. She had wanted to be with her all the time she was in Chicago, so they brought her down here. Her daughter came with her. That's when I first saw Napsie. I wrapped my arm around her, and I never took it away until she had to be put in the grave.

Diamond blue eyes. She was a beautiful girl. I used to tell her, "You got all the good looks and Anti didn't get any." She was Ismene and I, Antigone.

One night, I slept in the sheep and goat corral because their babies were being born. I had strived to get down there and did. They gave me some rags from home and I wrapped the babies in them so they wouldn't get cold. The mamas were trying to butt me out the whole time. Sometime, way past morning, I sat with my hands in my blonde mittens, and I heard someone say, "Yassou!", Greek for "Hello, friend!" That's what the goat herders in Greece used to say to other herders. People raised goats because the meat is like lamb. There were times when we didn't have much to eat. After the war years, WWI and WWII, everything became hard.

We started school in Belforest. It was a backwoodsman type of thing. There was just one road leading here, and we walked to school, taking shortcuts through the woods. It was three miles, and we had to make it on time. There was a lake we had to go around and a railroad track, an old-fashioned one that had been put out during the North-South War. That's how they got gunpowder and things. Little rails were laid out, stakes of thick wood, very wide, cut straight from trees. They were easy to ride on and were laid down in one district, then picked up and moved to another. The men wanted to get to the bay so they could fight the war. We would walk on those tracks, off the ground and away from snakes, through the swamp, to school.

As we started getting older, people began opening roads. Our school went to the seventh grade, and then children went to the eighth and ninth at Spanish Fort. Those past the ninth were either transferred to Bay Minette or Daphne. That's when the family decided we should go somewhere to advance our knowledge of words. We started at Daphne and, of course, they had to get us there. A family from Kansas came here, and they had an automobile, an Oberlin. Not many people had cars then.

There were three girls in the family. Mr. Malbis asked the father, "How much will you charge to take our girls with yours, like a school bus?" So they drove us to Daphne Normal School, Bessie, Napsie, and me. It was between the tenth and twelfth grades when they made things a little stiffer for you. Mr. Malbis said, "I think it would be better if these young ladies went to school in Mobile." We changed to the Convent of Visitation.

In the Convent, we had a room as big as two together, and the rooms were nicely done. They had some kind of curtain, of course they didn't have blinds in those days, something with a heavy lining that came down. There was a bathroom with stalls and showers. If we were playing games, we could come right in and get cleaned up for supper. But, in Catholic schools you have a lot of letters to do, and sometimes we had to study until ten o'clock at night. We were under the sisters' command. Sometimes I did little stinkies here and there, like most young people, but the thing I remember most about growing up is discipline. I got to be around fourteen years old before I realized the discipline had to be there. Of course, we were kept very much under their fingers at home.

I loved history and the English language. Miss Starkey is the one who instilled that in us. Even though

Mr. Malbis spoke Greek, he learned English from Miss Starkey. We would quote her the newspaper when we learned to read. She was always correcting us. "Don't talk like you've got a hot potato in your mouth," she would tell us. She ordered a book to teach you how to talk. You were to put your index finger in the roof of your mouth.

Miss Starkey was Irish. She came from South Dakota and settled in Foley. Her family had died, and the Starkey family had lost their son, so they adopted her. She worked on weekends to pay her tuition at the state college in Daphne, and she got a teacher's degree in Tuscaloosa. She was in her twenties when she came to Malbis. Her boyfriend wanted to get married before he went to war. She said, "No, if you go to the war and something happens, you'll have a hard time unwrangling all of it. You go to war, and I'll teach, and if everything works out…" Sure enough, he went and he did come back. He was one of the lucky ones. He took to driving a cab in Mobile and would bring it over sometimes on the ferry and pick us up. They never married. Miss Starkey was stubborn. Mr. Malbis used to call me stubborn. I said, "I'm the mule, but Miss Starkey is kicking me."

We had teachers before she came, but they were country and cooked ridiculous things like skunk, or is it possum? It's just like hog because it has lots of fat you have to remove and then cook it like a chop, beef, or lamb. The superintendent in charge came to Mr. Malbis and told him, "I got a lady teaching, and she is too much of a lady. The people at Spanish Fort are sort of uncultured. They don't speak well and wear their clothes a whole six months without taking them off."

When Miss Starkey first got to the school, she said, "I want everyone to come in a clean shirt." She bought them all longjohns, every child in the class. She paid for them out of her measly pay. It took a long time for people to like her. They called her "the foreigner." We were also called foreigners, and they laughed at us and made fun. So the superintendent advised she stay here and teach. Napsie and I were just six years old. She walked with us the three miles to school and held our hands all the way.

"Daddee" was our nickname for her. It is the name for the katydid that cricks all the time. When we were children, we put them in jars. Miss Starkey was always jumping around and cricking, too. We were her family and she became Greek Orthodox. Nano was her godmother. Miss Starkey had one sister-in-law who visited Malbis. She brought her grandchildren to the farm to play. They came every summer. One was named Martha. It was painful because we had to watch out for them. We had to see they had plenty to eat, to drink. They stayed in the house, upstairs with us, in one big open room with cots. The balcony was outside, and if they slept there, they had to have mosquito nets.

Miss Starkey took care of us and was responsible for the house. She kept up with people coming and going. Visitors came from all over. There are fourteen rooms and some slept on the porch under the nets. Of course, it made a lot of work for the women. There was much going on at home, and Mr. Malbis kept everyone so employed that no one dated or had boyfriends. Romances didn't start between the beautiful young Greek women because, for one thing, it was "hands off, no pity-pat". We were never without anything to do, and even though the community was self-contained, I never met so many people. Attorneys and judges from Mobile and all over the place stayed here. There were large, open spaces to shoot birds and rabbits, too. The visitors would hunt and bring back fifteen, sixteen quail and dove apiece.

PeeWee said there were turtles to hunt, also. Now I had eaten turtles at the Metropolitan Restaurant in Mobile and knew how delicious they were, but I wasn't going to let him roll one over on me. So, when PeeWee said, "Miss Anti, are we going to have turtles, too?" I said, "I know how to clean a crab, and I know how to clean a fish, but I don't know what to do with a turtle." "Well, I do," he said.

"They have fat in different places, and that's why sometimes they are so heavy they sink in the mud. They call them 'mud-diggers'."

The visitors liked to fish in Fish River. Mr. Malbis would say, "These ladies do too hard of work. You are going to clean and dress the fish for them to cook", and that's what they did. The pan we used for frying was very big. The table where we served was as long as a room and you'd walk around it and take what you wanted. We usually set it up in the yard but sometimes in the house. When the men hunted animals, they skinned them. The women didn't put up with that. It was the same with the fish.

When they brought fish back to the house, they needed to keep it cold. That is when the need for the ice plant came. Harry was in Chicago, then Paul, and they drafted Fred to go because he had a mechanical mind. There was a huge ice cream plant up there, and they were making and selling ice cream. They had become rich Greeks. Mr. Malbis asked if they would, as a courtesy, take these boys, and, of course, they did. After his stay, Fred returned and started the ice plant. We served all of Daphne, Belforest, and Spanish Fort. Malbis was in the middle. The men worked at the plant and at the little bakery with us. At four o'clock in the morning, we would get up and wrap bread by hand, like packages tied with string to hold them together. I was little, but I learned how to do that, tie the string without it coming unfolded.

This was about the time Pauline came. She was another adopted sister. Her father was a mason who came to Chicago from Greece. Mr. Tampas brought him here to help with construction for the new generation coming to the states. Pauline's mother had died. There were some nights and Saturdays when they put the big corrugated tub downstairs in front of the fireplace. They would heat the water in the laundry behind the kitchen. The ladyfolks and Pauline would wrap up Napsie and carry her down. I was on the stout side and no one would carry me. Sometimes it was cold, and I'd have to walk down the steps. My feet would be frozen, and I'd be glad to get in the tub.

I was about twelve, and during that time, I liked to jump rope. I would sing "Skip to My Lou, My Darling" and got where I could go two hundred. Then I broke my hip. Napsie and I were walking toward the cemetery, and there was a broken pipe, but no one could tell where it was. I found it, and it sliced me up good. They said they could hear me scream all the way to the nursery. They brought a doctor from Fairhope.

There is a picture they show a lot of Mr. Malbis. He looks like a missionary because of the hat. He didn't wear any such thing when he came over here, but he knew about them, and he knew what he had to do. He was not a minister, but he was religious, everything was religion. He wouldn't touch anything without taking out his yellow prayer beads. I never learned how to use them; I was doing well to keep up with my English. But he taught me to be spiritually constructive and work with my hands. We did hard work, but it needed to be done.

They used to bring a priest from Mobile, and he would do baptizing in the house. We put chairs together and a skirt with ruffles around it over a table. Water was placed on the table for christening. The house has some odd-sized rooms. A small bedroom could serve as two. We have the girls' dining room and the boys' dining room. Two parlors can open to the small room that served as a church for a time. Upstairs there are many bedrooms, and children didn't come downstairs except to eat and bathe. The smaller building was a library where I read. I liked that better than anything. We had a cellroom, a cellar type building, to store things so they wouldn't spoil. There we kept fresh onions. We even raised scallions. There are Greek onions called sheflins. When you get them clean, they stick on your fingers, and you have vinegar right there and put them in it. When you do, they turn a beautiful pink.

They cut timber and had turpentine. It took twenty-six years to pay off all the loans. But, little by little, with small businesses like the little bakery and dairy, we were able to do it. The big bakery was in Mobile and had a cafeteria downstairs. Mr. Malbis was progressive and said, "Save your money and something bigger and nicer will come from here". That is what happened with the Metropolitan Restaurant. A gentleman owned it, but he died on a trip to Greece. His widow had one child. She came to Mr. Malbis and asked him to buy the place. She said, "I'll fix some kind of contract with my lawyer. I am going to Greece to bury my husband. Can you have someone in the restaurant tomorrow morning?" Now who are you going to find by tomorrow? But, he did. They got the boys down there, lots of them had worked in the business in Chicago. You know, Mr. Phillip Pappas had a café in Chicago, and they had the hang of restaurants. They took it over.

We grew vegetables like okra and had a canning factory. The okra was brought in and had to be cured, steamed, and put into sterilized jars with Mr. Malbis' picture on the labels. He was wearing a red fez. On a trip, Mr. Malbis had met an Egyptian who practically fell in love with him. He called Mr. Malbis, "My Boy, My Boy."

31

The Egyptian asked him, "What have you done to keep your life straight?" Mr. Malbis said, "If you can't say something good, don't say nothing." They ended up putting together an international business and their connection lasted fifteen years. He wore the fez for the Egyptian.

Mr. Gregor went on a trip to China with Mr. Hercules. He sent me an organdy dress with a square neckline. I thought I was a little fatty, but I was tall enough to carry it well. It had a satin, blue sash, like children's clothes of the day, and I thought I looked nice. I wore that dress when Mr. Darwin came. At the time, he was trying to show that we come from monkeys, evolution. Mr. Malbis asked him, "How can a man like you, with all the training you've had, believe a human being could become a monkey or a monkey become a man? You can make a monkey act like a man, and sometimes we act like monkeys, but that is it."

We would take the ferry from Daphne to Mobile. In later years, there was something like a railroad, and beans and such were brought over on it. It took a long time to get things like manure. Fairhope had a big ferry, but ours was small. We had the Maypole Dances near the landing in Daphne. We wore big sunhats tipped over our eyes. They were made as costumes for Nicky Mallar's wedding. She had white roses, and it was the first time I had seen any. Of course, they came from Demeranville's Florist in Mobile.

They bought an old car and taught Angelo Matthews to drive. One day he was taking Mr. Malbis to the train station in Bay Minette, and a straggly dog kept crossing back and forth in front of them. The car overturned in the pond by the nursery. Our people and passersby came and got Mr. Malbis out of the water. By God's will there was a log in the pond, and when the car overturned, it got lodged under it. Mr. Malbis' face was below it, almost sea level, and his head got full of, you can imagine, all those pesky weeds and everything. As soon as they got him out, they sent him to a doctor in Fairhope. He was a good one, for nose and throat. He came from the East, and they had helped him get started here.

We never worked for outsiders. Miss Bessie worked for the little bakery, and I did too. But for two or three years, I had a job in Mobile. I learned to type and was fast, even without electric. They taught typing at the Daphne school, but I learned at home. My hip kept me at a desk job. I would sit with one leg up under the other. I had to wear elevated shoes that I bought in Mobile. They were expensive, $45.00 to $60.00 a pair. On Sundays, we would go to the Saenger Theatre for movies; it was the newest thing. In fact, you had to buy tickets ahead of time and pick them up early. Coming from Malbis, the people stayed at the Cawthorn Hotel.

Not only did Miss Starkey take care of the children and the house, she was Mr. Malbis' secretary. When she came here, she told him, "I will do anything that you want me to, and I mean that." She could form the words right, whereas he didn't have that kind of training. He had the kind that's in the brain. I used to listen to them, sitting in front of the fireplace, writing letters. She even negotiated some of the loans. She would say, "Mr. Malbis, you know I can't go there, to the bank, and talk to a man like that." He said, "You go there and tell them Mr. Malbis needs $400,000."

Mr. Malbis suffered from migraine headaches, and so did Miss Starkey. As a child, she had spinal meningitis, and that's why the Starkeys moved here, to get her away from cold weather. Mr. Malbis had the headaches because he had too much to do. He was the father of everybody. While the plantation was running, he was helping them out in Greece, too. Before World War II, he went to check on things. While in Greece, he had a garden and grew many things. Gardening was his hobby. He loved the smell of earth. He had a niece – she was young, but strong – who took olive oil and food for people to eat. She and Mr.

Malbis would have to act like spies because the war was beginning, and the Germans would take everything away. Mr. Malbis had the opportunity to get out and go to England but he did not take it. He stayed during the German occupation, and he got sick with colon cancer and died.

Mr. Malbis was a creative person and showed how innovative a group of people can be. One of the engineers in Mobile who had helped build The Panama Canal told Mr. Malbis, "We got to have more Greek people like you folks. Y'all are so creative. This is what Columbus did." Mr. Malbis had been dynamic, a true motivator.

Because of Miss Starkey's headaches, Dr. Goodard came from Mayo and brought a recipe for what she needed. He told her it was habit-forming and said for us to take it away when she didn't need it anymore. He wanted to put her in the hospital for one day, but she knew the place was cash-low and hard up for money because of the loans. When she was able, they sent her to rest in Greece. When she returned, the doctor said it would not be good for her to go back into the house with so many responsibilities. He said she would fall into the same pit. He said, "Do not expect her to come and live in this big house. You'll lose her soon." We bought her a small house in Fairhope and called it "The Wren". Napsie and I worked it out and brought the money from Mobile. We still had some notes to pay on it, and we did. We would go see her there and take Greek things she loved. Miss Lula, the one upstairs with paralysis, and some others made her favorite foods. She is buried here, next to the grave of my beloved, adopted mother. She lived a long time and gave so much love, I can't express it. Miss Starkey gave her everything to Malbis.

The people stayed together many years after Mr. Malbis died, but their lives were changing quickly. In another twenty years, it was over.

Bring that picture to my bed. It is in black and white, but Miss Starkey was wearing a dress of red and blue that day. I remember things the way they were.

LADIES ON THEIR BIRTHDAYS

We called my great-aunt Margaret "Bartie" even
though she said the familiarity of nicknames embarrassed
her. Her sister, my grandmother, made it up when they
were girls. Everybody used to think Bartie was smart.
Grandmother said that was why she never got married.
Bartie was the first in her family to go to college and even
studied in Europe for a while when she graduated. After
coming back to the states, or "off the continent" as she put
it, Bartie taught for many years at a boys' boarding school
up East. She spent the summers with us because, she said,
the folks up North didn't know how to have a proper
vacation. She said they had so many hobbies they couldn't
relax. Some of the students had to go to school all year
long. They didn't even know what summer was. I thought
Bartie was getting pretty tired of the North and I wasn't a
bit surprised the Labor Day she got lost in Virginia on her
drive back. When we heard about it, Grandfather sent his
chauffeur to Connecticut and brought her home for good.

She stopped driving then because, as Bartie said, she'd seen the world; what was there to see in Johnson, Alabama?

Grandmother had an apartment added onto the back of the house for Bartie. I spent most Sunday nights with her. During *The Ed Sullivan Show* we put our feet in tin washtubs she filled with water so hot I was afraid my skin would peel off and float to the surface. The Epsom salt she poured into it took some of the sting out, but our feet still turned red. She had a rule there was to be no talking during the program, not even commercials. She said the companies paid good money to advertise on America's favorite television show, and we could just sit there and learn something. After Ed Sullivan said goodnight, she turned the set off and closed the two oak doors to the TV-record player console. We talked about the places she had been in Europe and the people she had met. Switzerland sounded the best to me, and she said it was her favorite. She had friends there who sent cards every Christmas made from photographs the man took of snow-covered mountains near their home. I imagined myself with pigtails like Heidi's, on top of the Matterhorn. Bartie said she made snow ice cream over there that was better than ours. Grandfather gave her a heavy world atlas that she kept on the coffee table. She had it handy to settle arguments with him. She said he was too busy working to know what was what. In the atlas, she pointed out different countries she had seen, fifty in all. She had been to all fifty states, too. She was in Hawaii at a teacher's convention when it became a state. Over the television cabinet there was a picture of her with a group of ladies. They wore flowery dresses and had leis draped around their necks. I thought Bartie looked the best because she was the only one wearing a big, straw hat.

Although Bartie seemed fine to me, my grandparents thought she was looney, so they got a live-in nurse to keep an eye on her. Grandmother said she was afraid Bartie would hurt herself or burn down the house. She did leave the stove on a lot, even when she wasn't using it, and she burned most everything, which was a shame because she was a good cook. She was fond of sweets and was kind of famous in our town for her cookies and candy. The cooking stopped when the nurse came. But Bartie got me to stop at the Owl Drugstore on my way home from school on Mondays and charge a week's supply of Russell Stover French Mints to her. She said American candy was not good enough for us because we were worldly.

Bartie despised the nurse until Grandmother told her she was not her caretaker, but her houseguest. That pleased my aunt no end, and she started waiting on Carrie like she was the queen of England. She introduced me to her every time I came over. She wanted everybody to meet her company and once tried to get me to round up the neighbors for a party in Carrie's honor. Bartie was convinced they had met at the captain's table on a cruise of the Caribbean. She tried to teach us to play bridge with her because she enjoyed the game on the ship, but Carrie and I didn't much take to cards. Carrie thought they were "the devil's way". She liked to sit by the sunny window in the kitchen, perched high on the red stool Bartie kept to reach the tops of shelves. Carrie sat there for hours reading the Bible, which was torn at three corners and on most of the pages. Bartie said it looked like it was up to Scotchtape to hold together the Word of God. She and I sat in her living room most afternoons on the old, chintz sofa Grandmother had given her when she got a new, velvet one. We read aloud from my schoolwork and books she took out of the mahogany bookcase that had belonged to her mother. The television set wasn't turned on during the week. Bartie said it would ruin our eyes and spoil us for reading.

I think Bartie liked holidays even more than I did. She said she became a teacher because schools were the only businesses that knew how to celebrate. Halloween was my favorite, and she and I always dreamed up good costumes that Grandmother sewed. The best one was

Groucho Marx, and I won first prize for it at the church's costume party. I got to light a real cigar when I got home. Most of the other girls dressed as ballerinas and fairies. Bartie's favorite time was her birthday. No matter how much her mind started slipping, she never forgot that day. My birthday was three days before hers, so we had a special dinner together every year. She let me wear the diamond ring her mother left her and her gold broach to the dinners.

The year I turned fourteen and she seventy-six, Bartie didn't recognize anybody at the table but me, so I stuck by her all evening. Uncle George sat across the table from her. He sold cars for Mr. Finlay at the Chevrolet dealership. Mama said if it wasn't for his looks, he'd go broke because he couldn't sell a Rolls Royce to a sheik. Grandfather said customers had to beg Uncle George to sell them a car, and then he'd try to talk them out of it. Mama was right about his looks. I hoped he was serious about waiting for me to grow up so we could get married. He had the prettiest teeth I ever saw. He must have brushed them five times a day to get them so white. Bartie looked at Uncle George like it was the first time she'd ever seen him in her life and asked me, "Who is that good-looking man staring at me?"

Uncle George said, "You know me, Bartie. I've been hugging and kissing you all night."

"That's precisely why I was wondering who you are!" she said and threw me a look of righteous indignation as she crossed her hands over the folded napkin in her lap.

I had wanted fried shrimp for dinner, but Grandmother was on a diet. I don't know why she dieted – she looked skinny. She had worn a size four the year she and Grandfather spent in Washington, D.C. He was in charge of something to do with the lumber industry. Grandmother said she wanted to be buried in the ball gown she'd worn to Eisenhower's inauguration. I was afraid we'd be burying her sooner than she thought if she didn't start eating more. We had roast beef, boiled new potatoes, and asparagus.

Mama sat across from me. She had a perm in her hair that she'd gotten at Queen's Beauty Parlor. She said she was trying to get curly hair like mine so people would think we were sisters. I hated my hair. Sadie's daughter, Janie, promised to iron it for me. I wanted long, straight hair like the models in the magazines. If I ever got to meet the Beatles, I didn't want to have curly hair like the kid in "Peanuts".

Next to Mama, her date, Mr. Todd, sat perfectly straight. Grandfather said he didn't believe Mr. Todd's back had ever touched a chair. It was his first time at a family function, and he looked more nervous than ever. He kept running his long index finger up and down the side of his iced tea glass. His nails were so shiny I thought he used nail polish. I knew Mama would be mad later because nobody was talking to him, but every time I looked his way, he stared at me and gave me a fake smile. Mama caught me watching him and squinted her eyes at me. I'd never seen anybody attack their food with such vengeance, especially not boiled potatoes. They appeared so innocent under the thrashing of his knife and fork.

When it looked like everyone was finished with dinner, Grandmother put her foot on the pad under the table and produced a buzz in the kitchen, letting the cook know we were ready for service. I heard the swing door creak behind me as Sadie glided in on cue. She was wearing the French apron I'd seen wadded up in the refrigerator when I got milk for my cereal at breakfast. It had stayed damp with starch until she ironed it. Sadie was carrying a caramel cake on a crystal platter. The ivory candles were threatening to go out as she glided toward us. She set the billowing cake, our favorite, on the table between Bartie and me.

Behind their empty plates, everyone was anxiously waiting for dessert. My brother, Scott, was grinding the edge of his fork with the blade of his knife, a noise he knew made my fillings hurt. I was just about to reach behind Bartie and pop him on the shoulder when I noticed she was still eating. She took forever to finish. I told her to hurry up or I'd blow out the candles by myself and get all the wishes. She looked at me with watery eyes and I could see she was chewing as fast as her dentures would allow. Then Bartie's eyes opened wide with fear and her pale face became gray as she gasped for air. Mama told me to hit her on the back, but I was frozen. No one moved until Uncle George leaped around the table and jerked Bartie to a standing position. I dragged her chair out of the way and pushed her plate to the middle of the table, knocking her silver goblet onto Grandmother's best linen tablecloth.

Uncle George bent Bartie forward and encircled her back with his body as he put his arms around her and under her ribcage. Her head peeked out from under him. She looked like she was wearing a coat ten sizes too big. He yanked her little body twice, and a half-chewed piece of meat went flying out and onto my brother's plate, landing in his uneaten asparagus.

I turned Bartie's chair sideways to the table and she fell into it with a heavy sigh. I told her I guessed I'd go ahead and blow out the candles for both of us since they were dripping all over the icing. Grandmother started slicing the cake and placing the pieces on the green glass dessert plates Bartie had brought her from Venice. Grandfather said he didn't want any "Aunt Pearl" slice this year. Aunt Pearl, a relative famous for her stinginess, could cut cake so thin you could see through it.

I was watching a line of sweat run down the side of Mr. Todd's face and wondering why he didn't wipe it when Bartie turned to me again and asked, "Who is that handsome gentleman seated across from us? I think he is smitten with me."

"Bartie, you know Uncle George. He just saved your life. Don't tell me you have forgotten choking a few minutes ago."

"At the table, my dear? Never!"

I celebrate my birthday without Bartie now. She died during our birthday week over ten years ago. I still have caramel cake, even though I can't make it as well as Sadie. I put on an extra candle for Bartie and let her have one of my wishes.

LIVING WELL

Aunt Mallie was a witch, at least that's what everybody in town thought. Husbands threatened wives that they might turn out like her, mothers warned children to be good or she'd get them, and teenagers dared each other down the tree-shaded path to her house. Mallie stayed in an old shack beside the river, her nearest neighbor five miles away. She had been there for years with only cats to keep her company. Some said she ate live catfish from the river, wore no clothes, and kept alligators in bathtubs. Robert, the delivery boy at Sutton's Red Top, was the only person she ever saw.

Robert had been taking groceries to her once a week for twenty years. If it hadn't been for Aunt Mallie's orders, Mr. Schmidt said, he'd have to let Robert go. The store had quit making deliveries in the early eighties. Most folks went to the Piggly Wiggly on the bypass. They only stopped at the Red Top for last minute items like milk, bread, and cigarettes. Once the market that fed the town, the Red Top had become a convenience store. Mr. Schmidt's business was slow as Sunday drivers.

Robert was Mr. Schmidt's act of charity, hiring the handicapped. Robert was slow, mentally challenged it is called – dumb. He was sixty and had never worked anywhere but Mr. Schmidt's. He liked to think he had started at the Top. In his years of practice, he had gotten good at sweeping; there was never a mote of dust in the store, and the two plate glass windows stayed squeaky clean, allowing sunshine to pour in every morning, blanketing the cash register counter and Mr. Schmidt's desk, the only clutter in the place. Robert knew each item on every shelf, dusted all the cans, boxes, and bags. He kept the shelves color-coded. Cans of tomatoes sat beside beets, ketchup, cranberry juice, and cherries. Below them were turnips, spinach, lentils, and sour apple candy. The lower shelf held napkins, powdered milk, mashed potatoes, grits, and toothpaste.

The few customers who came in knew Robert and spoke to him. He'd grin and grunt a "morning" or "afternoon", sometimes getting the two mixed up in his embarrassment at being noticed. Everybody seemed to like him. Mr. Schmidt said many times that he should run for mayor. He was the most popular fellow in town, a good listener.

Aunt Mallie said so too, when he delivered her groceries. Every week she ordered the same things, putting the list in his hand as he departed after leaving a pound of chicory coffee, a box of Bisquick, a large bag of Meow Mix, seven Cokes, one pound of sugar, a carton of brown eggs, a gallon of whole milk, and two gallons of Barber's vanilla ice cream. She liked Barber's because it was a local product, said Alabama ice cream was the best in the land.

Robert went to her place on Tuesday afternoons, after the milk truck made the delivery to the store. Mr. Schmidt let him take the 1954 Chevrolet pickup even though he didn't have a license. Mr. Schmidt said a fool couldn't hurt that truck. Robert liked driving, and he always went full speed, forty miles an hour. It didn't take him long to go the fifteen miles to Mallie's, unless it was raining, then the windshield wipers didn't work right. They were on a vacuum compressor and moved slowly and not at all up hills or if the headlights were turned on.

When Robert arrived at Mallie's blue cabin, she was standing at the backdoor with a big, red umbrella if it was raining or an old army blanket to throw over his shoulders if it was cold. She'd come out to the truck and walk with him as he carried the brown paper bags, holding open the screen door that had no screen in its bottom half. Neither of them talked as they set to work putting the groceries on pine planks that served as shelves in her tiny kitchen, a room where Robert felt cozy. He liked the potbellied, wood-burning stove in the corner and the old refrigerator that wore its motor on top like a hat. He especially liked the way Mallie had papered the walls with magazine pictures of cats and photos out of *Country Living.* Before he arrived, she set the green linoleum table with two yellowed, but freshly starched and pressed napkins, metal tablespoons, and blue and white ironstone bowls.

After the supplies were put away, Mallie asked Robert to join her for an afternoon dessert. She gently knocked off three or four cats who huddled on top of the Sears chest freezer and brought out a gallon tub of Barber's vanilla. She said the cats stayed on top of the deep freeze because that's where she kept the fish she caught in the river, and they knew it. She spooned out three scoops for Robert and two for herself. Then she took the warmed, tin pot of drip coffee off the woodstove and poured thick brown coffee over the ice cream.

They ate in silence, Robert finishing before Mallie was through with one scoop. He pushed his bowl toward the center of the table, and Mallie said, "You're not going so soon, are you? Stay a while and let's talk. A person gets a bit lonesome out here, you know." He did know. Mallie was the only one he ever talked to. He didn't count Mr. Schmidt. They went whole days without a word; things had gotten pretty routine at the store.

Robert figured he knew Mallie better than anybody. They'd been talking for many years. She told him about her husband, Judson. It was love at first sight and they had married at eighteen. Mallie was the prettiest girl in Wilcox County; everybody said so. At first, her parents didn't think Judson was good enough for her because he sold cars and was from Louisiana, but they did admire the green Buick he drove, brand-new, and the only convertible in three counties. When he purchased the dealership at twenty-four, they were beside themselves with pride and accepted him like their own son.

Mallie made Judson's breakfast at four-thirty each morning, and he was at work by half past five. She ran the ten-room house with a maid and gardener. She grew a vegetable patch and the finest hybrid tea roses in town. She studied piano from old Mrs. Toulmin who came to her house on Wednesday mornings and, afternoons, she took her easel and painted water colored landscapes of the countryside. They had late dinners because Judson came in from the office around seven. He thought he should be available to customers weekends and holidays, so nights were the only time she had with him. She worried about his health and tried to talk him into taking a short trip to his brother's place in Florida, but he wouldn't hear of it. He said relaxing made him nervous, and the mosquitoes on the coast would probably give him malaria.

Judson had a stroke at the office. Mallie sat at the upright Steinway struggling with "The Battle Hymn of the Republic" when the ringing of the telephone began on the hall table. It was Thursday, maids' day off all over town, with afternoons so quiet most of the stores closed at noon. When Mallie lifted the receiver to her ear, she heard Inez whispering. She had trouble deciphering what her husband's secretary, who usually spoke in such a loud voice you had to hold the receiver at arm's length, was saying. Mallie caught the word "hospital" and dropped the earpiece, letting it dangle – Inez still breathing her words into it.

After wolfing down a hamburger Inez had brought him from Roy's Drive-In, Judson had taken his customary cigar break. He was leaning back in his brown, leather chair, front legs off the floor, when his secretary heard him fall. She rushed in and found him silent, staring up at her, gripping his chest with both hands. She called the ambulance, and it arrived within eight minutes, rushing him to County Memorial where Doctor May met him. When Mallie arrived, she flew down the corridor of the one-story building, lips moving in a continuous prayer. The doctor was standing outside the door to the emergency room, speaking in a hushed voice to his nurse. Mallie knew it was bad when he turned to face her, eyes filled with regret at not being able to work a miracle. The stroke had been severe, and there was scarred tissue causing Dr. May to suspect there had been one or two earlier, smaller ones, which Judson had ignored.

Judson stayed at the hospital three weeks, enduring physical therapy to restore limbs that refused to be revived. The doctor told Mallie there was nothing more he could do and the patient was discharged. Mallie brought her twenty-eight year old husband, paralyzed on his left side and no longer able to walk or talk, back to the house he had barely known. After several months of lying on his back, staring at the ceiling, Judson gave up hope of returning to work and waited for his permanent vacation to end. He never got out of bed and died within six months.

Mallie talked to Judson's nephew, John, at the dealership and asked him to take over the company. It was a decision she made with hesitation because John's wife caused him a lot of problems. Suzanne was high-strung, from old money. She could not accept living in a country town surrounded by nothing but pine trees and pastures. She'd been the queen of Mardi Gras in New Orleans and had a twelve by ten foot oil painting of herself wearing a beaded gown and train to show for it. The painting dwarfed their house in Rolling Hills. To Suzanne, the house was downright tacky, like using paper napkins with your good china. Not to mention that Suzanne had sofas and chaise lounges, fourteen in all, in the U-Store-It, You-Lock-It. She told John they were lucky they hadn't been robbed by some of their middle class neighbors. She said they needed a new place, something that suited them, and was elated when he became manager. It meant more money. She went to New Orleans the first week after his promotion and hired an architect. She wanted a miniature Tara. She dreamed of being Scarlett.

A few years later, when she and a decorator from Atlanta had the house the way Suzanne wanted it, she found she was pregnant, a most unattractive state she thought. She bore twins, Jon and Jamie, and referred to them as the biggest mistake of her life, times two. She never forgave the boys for ruining her perfect, size six figure. As they grew, they made her so nervous she quit playing the violin in the afternoons, her one luxury, and started drinking earlier, to calm her nerves. Before the twins came, she wouldn't have touched a drop before five.

John worried about money. The new house cost three times what the architect had suggested. Thank goodness he had talked Mallie into letting him borrow from the company to pay for it. Suzanne told him he knew she was expensive when he married her. The bills were growing faster than his paycheck; he wasn't able to put anything aside. He thought about money all day, doodling figures on the pad at his desk while three salesmen worked the fewer and fewer customers who drifted into the showroom.

The bank called Mallie when the company debt wasn't being met. She realized talking to John wouldn't help. He was over his head in problems. She didn't need a big place anymore, so she decided to raise some money by selling her house, a three-story Victorian with turrets and balconies, which was later torn down to make way for a Walmart shopping center. Mallie put the money into the dealership and moved to a piece of property she and Judson had on the river. She had always said she wanted to live on the water.

Mallie would have liked to help Suzanne with the boys, but their mother didn't want them hanging out at the river. She said it wasn't a clean place for them. She expected her children to be knights for Mardi Gras when they were old enough. Her biggest dilemma was that they couldn't both be king. She wasn't sure how they'd pay for it, but knew John would find a way.

No one expected it, least of all Suzanne, when John didn't go to the office one Friday morning in July. He was never heard from again, just erased from the town. The boys were working offshore in Louisiana. It was the summer after high school graduation, and neither had shown any inclination to go to college. Suzanne had fallen asleep on the blue, crushed velour sofa, her favorite, the night before, after watching *Sunset Boulevard* on late night TV. When she awoke, she cleaned out three filthy ashtrays, placed the wine glasses in the dishwasher, and fixed cereal for her husband and a Bloody Mary for herself. When John kissed her goodbye at the front door, ashes from her cigarette fell on the shoulder of his pale blue shirt. He complained that she needed to flick them before they grew so long. The last time she saw him, he was going down the front steps, stopping to pat one of the massive, limestone columns holding up the porch roof.

Saturday, around midday, Inez from the office called Mallie and told her John hadn't been to work in two days. Mallie got the town's sole taxi to take her to Suzanne's. She found her niece dressed in a gold, sequined Mardi Gras ball gown, passed out on a sofa in the back hall near the kitchen. The hem of the dress was ripped and torn in places to her knees, and Suzanne was covered in mud. Since three that morning, she had been riding the old, white thoroughbred they kept in the side pasture. She had even set up jumps and put him through them.

A month later Suzanne, dressed in her queen's gown with the rhinestone crown upon her head, walked out to the barn and lay down on scattered hay. She placed the tip of John's rifle in her mouth, resting the oily metal on her tongue. The silk and satin skirt embroidered with seed pearls rustled as she pulled her right leg from underneath and stretched it along the cold barrel until her big toe reached and pushed the trigger.

Suzanne's body was discovered by the handyman, and the news was all over town by noon. Mr. Schmidt let Robert borrow the truck to tell Mallie.

The two old friends sat across from each other at the kitchen table. Mallie smiled as a tabby cat leaped from the floor onto her lap. She rubbed the black stripes behind his ears as he kneaded her left thigh with his paws.

"I guess I'm not surprised about Suzanne, Robert. She was like a hothouse rosebud, the kind you buy from the florist. It is picked early and not meant to bloom. The color is strong, but there is no fragrance. It's a shame, but most people just don't know how to live."

Robert looked at his spidery hands spread across the table where a bowl of ice cream usually sat.

DIXIE WHISTLES

"I know 'bout New York City, the Big Apple. I was one of them New York slicks. Ain't nothing I don't know 'bout that city. I stayed 'round Harlem." The small, wrinkled black man spoke with the stub of a fat cigar clenched between his teeth. His tone was gruff and his words sounded like they tumbled over gravel on the way out.

The old man was standing between the front seats, straddling the aisle of the Amtrak car. A boy of five was sitting on the seat to his right, fidgeting with a "Transformer". The man leaned like he had a catch in his back toward the child and asked him, in a loud voice, where he was going. The boy didn't look up from his toy and mumbled a short response. The man stood up straight, hand on his lower back, and said to the rest of us, blacks and whites gathered in the train's rows of old, cracked leather seats, "The boy don't know where he's going. He don't know where he's from."

The boy looked at the old man through squinted eyes, shaking his shaved head like he thought the man a fool. "I do, too. I'm from New York City." His traveling companion, his grandmother, whispered in his ear to remember what she had told him about lying. He then said, "My mother lives in New York City, and so do I. She," he said pointing to his grandmother, "don't know where I'm from."

The old man recognized competition when he met it and stepped forward a little, toward his captive audience. He wore a pale, blue shirt with faded vertical stripes and tiny bouquets of violets scattered across it. It was more like a baby's flannel blanket than a man's shirt. With this, he had a navy tie of horizontal, beige stripes loosely knotted at this throat. The necktie looked like it would have been more comfortable next to a Brooks Brother's suit. His pants were khaki cotton and bunched at the bottom because they were too long for him. Brand new, white tennis shoes completed the outfit.

His wife sat beside his empty seat, a small, thin woman dressed in black. Her hair was held back from her face in a hairnet. She was silent, her eyes fixed on the back of the seat in front of her, and you could tell she was used to listening. The man soon lost interest in speaking to the group and dropped with a heavy plop into the space beside her.

I went back to reading my book and would have forgotten about him, but I saw him two hours later in what served as the train's dining car. It had lost its luxury long ago and had become more of a traveling lounge than a diner. The passengers were sitting at tables eating bags of salted peanuts and drinking alcohol from the bar that ran down the side of the room. The old man had a can of Budweiser in his left hand and used his right to emphasize his opinions to a black woman I'd seen drinking beer in there three hours before when I was looking for the restroom. They were talking politics – the state elections were in two weeks – in voices that got louder with each sentence.

I left and returned to my seat, passing his wife sitting in the same pose she had maintained all day. The only thing different was that she had exchanged the hairnet for a white beret. I thought she could be a broken statue en route to the Museum of Natural Agony. With her right toe, she was kicking the bottom cushion of the empty seat in front of her. She kept the rhythm of that constant thudding throughout the trip.

At the car's head, the little boy, Johnny, sat on the floor. He was driving a beat-up model car around Granny's feet, stopping to gas up with one of her shoelaces. His grandmother read the newspaper and pretended not to notice. He hummed softly to himself as he maneuvered the toy car over the brown hills of the toes of her shoes, into the valley between them, and around the hairpin turns at her heels. I sat in the seat across from them, closed my eyes, and relaxed, letting his voice pour over me like warm milk.

The beer-drinking woman from the dining car huffed in and fell like an anchor into her seat behind the boy and his grandmother. She wore a navy cap with sparkles and a red, white, and blue shiny dress that was two sizes too small. She spoke to her friend, Angel.

"That's the biggest mess I've ever seen. That many educated people and nobody in charge." She was disgusted with the diner because they had run out of light beer.

I wondered where the old man was. I pictured him still waving around his warm beer can and pontificating politics to anyone who would listen while his wife sat, kicking, and staring ahead.

Angel and her friend started discussing selling timber and how much money was in the trees passing outside our windows. They were talking about ways to develop land and build houses.

"You can see blue ribbons on trees. That's telling you something," said Angel to her friend, who was adding figures on a small notebook she had pulled from a large vinyl bag at her feet.

Johnny was singing to himself. He was in his seat now, sitting on top of his old brown suitcase. His left arm was in a cast and he leaned it, at an angle, against the cold window, letting the stream of air conditioning run up the narrow space between plaster and arm. The panes were polka-dotted with raindrops; it had been raining off and on all day. The train let out a low, even whistle to warn creatures it was coming through. The whistle was so long you could almost see it racing ahead of the train. The spring green woods were dappled with white oatleaf hydrangeas, and pink and peach buds were popping out on other bushes.

When we got to the Evergreen depot, Angel and her friend got up, gathered five heavy bags between them, and went out into the rain. They were new to the area. They had come from the city to tell relatives what to do with their uncle's land. Before we arrived, they asked me, "Evergreen got a station?" They do, but not much else. Trains stop at a lonely old building right in the middle of town divided by tracks that separate the races.

Johnny and Granny got off too. I was sorry because I knew I would miss the comfort of his music. He said, "Bye, bye" to me as they got two cardboard boxes, his suitcase, and her old, leather bag together and departed. We'd had a lot of eye contact during the daylong trip, but those were the first words to pass between us. I was glad he was the first to speak. Johnny was a kind boy, and I hoped he would grow up that way.

The old man returned to his seat, smoking a fresh cigar and carrying drinks for himself and his patient wife.

"The further you go, the later you get," he said in a voice meant for all of us. "But y'all don't know what I'm talking 'bout. Computer stuff, understand?" His wife leaned toward him and suggested in a whisper that he quiet down, there were people sleeping. His voice still booming, he lamented that he was only able to bring two plastic cups from the dining car. According to Alabama law, if he'd had a paper sack, he could have brought a canned beer. "You can drink a can," he said to his wife.

From the back of the car, a white woman asked him, "You must have worked on a train. Have you?"

"Forty-five years," he said. "I'd a been educated 'cept for that. Got a girl with child. Had to work." Then he started mumbling into his cup about being a minister, four-year studies, intern a year under a pastor.

"What denomination?" asked a white man in another back seat.

"I'm Luther," he said and started talking about his belief in being chosen for the Lord. His wife wanted to drink in silence. She was disgusted with his incessant conversation and sucked in her jaws with a loud sigh.

"Rough road," he said. No one knew what he meant. "I'm just a lay minister. I can do all but two things – give communion and perform marriage. I can bury you, but not marry you." He stood facing the white group in the rear of the car, leaning against the back of the seat in front of him. "Birmingham is my home. I'm on my way to Mobile for a funeral."

Brewton rolled past, and I looked out and thought about the beauty of my state. We were in its heart on the train. Cars show you nothing but highways. Trains serve the countryside like Thanksgiving dinner.

"People want to get rich right away," he continued while his wife made clicking noises, her tongue against her teeth. "Some people have a long life, some die young. My daddy lived to be ninety-six, and he did both, drink and smoke. I had a brother did neither and died at twenty-seven."

The white passengers commiserated among themselves with like stories.

"You can find exceptions to everything," said a prim lady in pink with gray hair pulled tight in a French twist.

The preacher ignored her. "I smoke cigars and drink all my life. Two, three, four cigars a day. How old would you say I am?"

"Late sixties," said a fat man in plaid shorts.

"Seventy-two," said the man's equally fat wife in an excited voice that made you think she was a game show contestant.

"I'm ninety-two. 1907." he said. "I been retired twenty-two years. 1973. I think that's 'bout right. And last night I had one of the best sleeps of my entire life. I didn't wake up 'til 5:00. A clean conscience, that'll keep away insomnia."

His wife sat still, gritting her teeth, hands folded like old, soiled linen across the Good Book on her lap. She was tired – Bible weary – and closed her eyes. She thought about Charlie, the man she almost ran off with when she was nineteen. Her parents didn't approve because he didn't attend church and she hadn't wanted to disappoint them. She wondered what Charlie's life was like. She pictured him standing at a grill in his backyard, grandchildren running and laughing in the distance, his wife sitting in a plastic chair nearby. They talked of times past, smiling at each other as they recalled the good old days.

FORMING HABITS

I married at twenty-two, not because I was in love, but because I didn't know what else to do. Six months earlier my mother had asked me to come home from Aunt Charlotte's house and talk about my future, since I had graduated from college and had secured no job with my geology degree. She and I argued over the telephone. Although I was unsure what I should do, I didn't want to sell real estate like she and her husband suggested. She begged me to come back and talk to her and promised that my stepfather would not be involved. My aunt's beach house had been my cocoon since school, and I left with a feeling of vulnerability. She had four children, and her vacation home was filled with people joking and laughing. My twin brothers had been sent to boarding school when they were twelve, and I had been threatened with living with my aunt. Like most of my mother's threats, it had no follow-up, and I had to settle for visits.

Still wearing her thick, auburn hair in a prominent bun at the nape of her neck, Mother greeted me at the door with one of her non-touching hugs that leaves you feeling dirty instead of comforted. She led me to her upstairs bedroom at the back of the house. On the hall walls we passed gilt framed pictures of my brothers and me. When I entered the room, my stepfather slammed the wooden door shut behind me. He stood between me and it – even a short man has more strength than a woman. He commanded I lower my jeans, a ratty pair with patches covering holes, and pushed me face down on the bed. With one hand, he unlatched the silver buckle of his brown leather belt, and I heard a familiar whir as it ripped through its loops, the metal of the buckle slightly clanking as his cigar shaped fingers tightened around it. With his other hand, he held the back of my neck and pinned me to the mattress. Mother leaned against feather pillows at the head of the Mallard bed she'd inherited from her New Orleans grandmother. She cradled her knees and watched in silence. The belt came down hard, slapping my bare bottom and thinly covered back. Twice the buckle came free in his hand and tore into the exposed skin of my buttocks, leaving its red imprint on pink skin. I was thankful it did not hit my back because bruises there were slow to heal and hurt for a long time; butt lashes only stung for a couple of days. When he leaned back to catch his breath, I reached to my knees, pulled up my pants, turned, opened the door, and ran out of their house.

I never returned. Within six months, I married a boy I had gone out with four or five times. He had deep green eyes and was the first quiet redhead I'd ever met. He had started his own business, a neighborhood hardware store. He had been a soldier in Viet Nam, and I was captivated by the harsh stories he told of dying comrades and guards so high on drugs they couldn't look out for their men. He seldom smiled, and his laugh sounded hollow. He followed a strict diet with no sugar, salt, or white flour, but he didn't approve of my being a vegetarian. He liked rock climbing, weight lifting, and running marathons. He enjoyed pushing himself to exertion to see how much his body could take. I preferred trips to the beach, riding horses in the country, reading, and the arts. I was proud of my sense of humor, but he told me I was the only one who laughed at my jokes. I thought he didn't laugh because he couldn't, and I was young enough to think I could teach him to be happy and that our differences would enhance the relationship. But the arguing never stopped. I wanted to be a good wife and decided patience was the quality of which I was most in need. It comes with age, and most people find it if they wait long enough, but I was in a hurry, so I took up knitting.

Classes were offered in a small brick building in a shopping area so close to our house that I could walk. I had been married for a year and was four months pregnant when I started. Every morning from ten to twelve, five women came to Katie Griffin's Knit Shop and sat at a round table with their work in progress in front of them, gathering instruction and tips from one of the two owners who also sat at the table. Two of the women were Holocaust survivors and their numbered tattoos peeked out from under long sleeves as delicate pale fingers flittered like hummingbird wings over their work. Their accents were strongly German and their faces hard unless they spoke of grandchildren. I sat across from them, but they didn't talk to me. I hoped to teach my hands such control, but they might as well have been coated with butter.

One of the other knitters befriended me, said I reminded her of her granddaughter in Vermont. I sat in the straight-back chair next to her, and she helped me when the teacher was busy instructing others. I needed constant supervision and had to pull out almost every stitch. While everyone else chatted away to the rhythm of their needles, I sat silently with complete concentration, pushing my needle into the yarn and trying to catch the loop to pull it back through and off the other needle, knit and purl, knit and purl. The ladies used metal needles of various colors that indicated size while I clodded along on big wooden ones. They reminded me of the crayons first graders use, and I knew I was working with them because their rubbing together made a less annoying thud than the sharp clicks I would have created on aluminum needles. Synthetic threads were like tiny razors that ripped your fingers with hair thin cuts; wool was gentler. We used heathers from the British Isles, colors that reminded you of the sea from Scandinavian countries; naturals, dark browns, and blacks from Australian sheep; and giddy-colored, thin cords from South America. There were some cottons from which to choose, but not many, although in the years to come there would be chenilles and even silk yarns. We stuck with the wools. Within a few months, I developed calluses on my fingers from the constant rubbing against the needles.

My first project, a pale, yellow sweater for the baby I was expecting, was a simple cardigan with raglan sleeves and the teacher, whose improbable name was Dinky, taught me to knit-in little ducks of my own design bordered by pink bands that wrapped around the shoulders. I was more proud of that sweater than anything I had ever accomplished, and I finished it the week the baby arrived. Of course, I dressed her in it when we left the hospital, no matter that the September weather was eighty degrees.

After that, I started knitting all the time – baby sweaters for my child and those of friends. There were sweaters with the alphabet, trains running around them, every possible farm and zoo animal, "stop" on the front and "go" on the back, names across the chest, and scenes from nursery rhymes. Then I started knitting for my family, sending them packages at Christmas and birthdays filled with all types of sweaters and vests, argyle socks, mittens, muffs, and scarves. It was as if I were outfitting the Allied Troops during World War II. It never crossed my mind that it was too hot in Laurel, Mississippi, for all those woolens. We were in Madison and, although it was Alabama, to me it was like living in Ohio.

I took the baby with me to the knit shop in the mornings and knitted in the afternoons while she slept. At night, I knitted while my husband watched TV. He was the only person I knew who didn't have one of my creations. He said he hated sweaters; they were feminine, and he wouldn't be caught dead in one. On the baby's second Christmas, when my husband opened his gift from me, he let out a sigh of relief when he saw the sleeping bag. "Thank God," he said, "I was afraid it was something you'd made."

There was more ripping out than actual going forward when I began, so I got used to the idea that no

70

mistake was permanent. Knitting made me brave. I could see for the first time in my life that, although I made errors, they could be corrected; there was hope if I would endure. With every article I completed, my self-confidence grew. In the beginning, my husband had encouraged me to take up the hobby to get me out of his hair. But, with every stroke, I felt better about myself, and he grew to hate it.

Thursday nights the local theatre showed art and foreign films, and I engaged a babysitter on a weekly basis so we could see them together. He preferred movies about Viet Nam, and when we attended those, the violence sometimes made me run to the bathroom and throw up. I started knitting during the war movies. Without looking at my work, I could feel my way through and imagined myself a blind woman building something she would never see. On the drive home from the theatre, we rode in silence. I wanted to discuss what we had seen, but he said there was no point in recreating shows the directors had already made. I grew tired of arguing. I quit calling him at work when he accused me of being a clinging vine. I stopped getting up and having breakfast with him, and our sex life deteriorated to the point that he sent me to a psychiatrist. He thought I was losing my mind because I didn't enjoy giving him oral sex every night, his pressing my head down on his penis until I swallowed his sperm.

He said the whores in Viet Nam admired his big organ and fought over who would have it. They gave him herpes in return, and I developed it on my nose.

We both started drinking too much, but only on weekends. He thought the five-day fast would keep us from becoming alcoholics. My drinking usually led to crying, and he said it made him sick at his stomach to see my loss of control, so I ended most Saturday nights sitting on the tiled bathroom floor sobbing into my hands to muffle the sound. He was a silent drunk, and the only emotion he showed was anger. The first time he scared me was the night he threw the telephone at my head because he said I talked too much. He jerked it off the bedside table, and the plug cracked as he ripped the cord from the outlet. The handset and base stayed as if glued together when he hurled it through the air. It whizzed past my head, close enough to blow the hair from beside my ear. The window shattered onto the wooden floor as the phone went through and landed with a crack on the pavement below. All I would let myself think about was cleaning up the glass. I went to the kitchen to get the broom as he stomped out of the house.

Six or seven months later, I was pregnant with our second daughter and in the nursery fixing a crib for her when my husband came home from a meeting of the

Humane Society. I hadn't been able to get a babysitter for our two-year-old, and he was angry that he'd had to go alone. He had been to a bar with some of his friends after the meeting. He said it pissed him off to see those idiots making more money than he did. He walked over to the side of the baby bed and, without speaking a word, struck me on the left side of my face, sending my glasses flying and knocking me to the floor. That night I made up my mind to leave after the baby arrived and told the psychiatrist of my decision at my Tuesday appointment. He said he had wanted to suggest it for a year, but I had to be the one to decide. He offered to help me get through the divorce, but said it would not be necessary for me to continue treatment after that. I felt guilty because my husband had paid seventy-five dollars an hour for these sessions that he believed would make me desire him.

I felt obligated to let my mother and stepfather know their first grandchildren, so we spent Easters, Christmases, and birthdays at their lake house. When the children didn't need me, I faced the brick fireplace in their pine-paneled living room and knitted. I floated on a peaceful cloud in the upholstered Queen Anne chair with sides high enough to hide my face and only the click of my needles and the crackle of the fire to disturb the silence. Mother and my stepfather adored my husband. They liked his quiet manner, thought it indicated intelligence. My husband admired my stepfather and his ability to make money, and my stepfather liked the way he listened to his ideas without interruption. Because of his confidence in my husband's business abilities, my stepfather decided to open a branch of his grocery store chain in Madison and let him run it. We talked it over, and I told my husband I was opposed to the idea because they would interfere in our lives. He chose to take the job anyway, and I knew it was time for me to leave.

I should have been the one to tell Mother and my stepfather that I was divorcing my husband, but I was afraid of what they might say and do. It didn't surprise me when they called from a local motel saying my husband had told them of my foolish idea and that I was to come within the hour and discuss it. After depositing the children with a neighbor, I drove downtown as slowly as possible, parked in the most distant spot in the lot, walked up four flight of stairs instead of taking the elevator, and knocked with a shaky fist on the door to their room. They looked bigger than usual standing together in front of the picture window and looking out. I knew they had watched my arrival. They told me to sit on one of the two beds and I stiffened my body in preparation for what was to come. Mother walked over to me and slapped my face before they took turns screaming. I sat still, trying to keep my feelings a secret, seeing them through soft-focused eyes, searching for something that wasn't there. I prayed to feel love for them because I thought I was supposed to, but no feelings came. They told me I was crazy and needed to talk to a psychiatrist. When I told them I had been seeing one for years and that he supported my decision, they suggested I see a priest. We were Presbyterian, but everybody knew where Catholics stood. Then they accused me of leaving for another man. They could not understand my throwing away a husband who had all the attributes they admired – a man just like them.

I left, biting my lower lip and holding tears inside until I was safe in the sanctuary of my car. When I got home, I started a gray cable stitch pullover for myself. To retain the pattern while spacing the twisted rows, cables require closer attention than other sweaters. It was the first and last one I attempted, but I needed to prove that I could do it.

For the next few months, my husband and I lived in silence except for my pleading with him to leave. He refused to go, said I was unstable and unable to know what was best. I talked to his brother, and when he suggested my husband move out, he did. We were the first of our friends to divorce, and neither of us knew what to anticipate. Finalities are never what anyone expects. I asked for the children and half of the proceeds from selling the house that Aunt Charlotte had helped us buy. A year later my children and I were living on Lake Pontchartrain in a quiet community without a knit shop.

FLAG WAVING PROUD

"Kimberly went to Atlanta this week. You know, interviewing for some big corporate job. She has her mind set on being a CEO," said Miriam. She touched the smooth edge of the Styrofoam cup to her glossy red lips and felt the steam go up her nostrils before the hot liquid struck the tip of her tongue. She thought she smelled plastic and wondered if her friend, Cindy Rose, had been correct when she said she'd read that one-tenth of the Styrofoam in every cup melted in hot liquid. People all over America were drinking polymer and cellulose for breakfast.

"That girl of yours is such a whiz. My Donna is still at LSU. Can you believe that? Sometimes I wish she'd just gone into business or even real estate like my husband's brother's girl. She makes good money. This law school stuff sure has been a drain on me and her daddy. Pass me the Sweet n' Low, honey," said Charlene.

Shelia spoke up. "By the time she was seventeen, Mary Fay had realized her aspirations. She'd reached all the goals she had in mind." Shelia sat at a table in the corner so she could smoke Kools. Although they all used to smoke, now the others didn't approve. She laid the morning edition of the *Mobile Press Register* someone had left in the break room on the laminated table and picked up her Coca-Cola.

"How is Mary Fay? Wasn't she a cheerleader in high school? Such potential," said Miriam as she tore a chocolate glazed doughnut in two. She was watching her weight, so she never ate more than half.

"Mary Fay's got herself a teller job over at AmSouth. Been there three weeks and she's already counting on big retirement. If she don't start getting there on time, she'll be retiring before she knows it. Don't ask me what somebody that thinks two plus two equal three doing with other folks' money no ways." Shelia twisted the tip of her Kool around the edge of the tin ashtray in front of her.

"Why, I thought Mary Fay had married one of the Richmonds from Robertsdale. What's she doing working?" Miriam turned her head away from Shelia to avoid cigarette smoke being blown in her face by the overhead air conditioning vent.

"Mary Fay's been divorced. I could have told anybody who'd asked that marriage wasn't gonna work. Him and his high-falooting people. His mama thinks she's the Queen of Sheba and, can you believe it, she ain't but from up around Opp somewhere. No, that marriage was a dead end from the word go." Shelia stabbed out her cigarette.

"What happened, honey? I mean, if you don't mind my asking." Charlene glanced at Miriam.

"Well, Lord knows the blame ain't partial to the Richmonds. Mary Fay sure put in her share. The straw that finally broke the camel's back was when Danny – that's the boy – came home one night and pushed Mary Fay across the living room, right up to the big screen TV they'd bought with the checks they got as wedding gifts. The next day Mary Fay came home bawling, saying she was a battered wife and all that. The boy didn't really do nothing to her and, if you ask me, he was probably provoked. I think she was more afraid he'd break the television than hit her. Divorced at twenty-two. Don't that beat all."

"My Kimberly is not going to settle down until she's secure in her job and well established in Atlanta," said Miriam, a proud flush crossing her cheeks.

"When will that be, sugar?" asked Charlene, a thin smile on her lips.

"Well, it ain't entirely Mary Fay's fault that her situation in life is not working out. When she was in high school, flag-waving was that girl's dream. She'd practice for hours on end in the back yard with them flags. Her daddy even installed one of those sensor lights – you know, the kind that come on when you walk past 'em – so she could practice after dark. Only problem was she moved around so much, waving those flags, the thing flicked on and off half the night. Nearly drove the neighbors crazy." Shelia pulled another Kool from the half empty pack in her lap. She liked to have three during the morning break.

"It seems I remember seeing her at some of the football games. You know Kimberly dated the quarterback, Earl Williamson. That boy was sure crazy about Kim," said Miriam as she dabbed a paper napkin at some doughnut crumbs in the corner of her lips. If she dabbed instead of wiping, she was able to keep most of her lipstick intact. "She looked real smart in the little tiger suit she wore."

"Yeah, Mary Fay was proud of that uniform alright. She made me iron it before each game. I never saw the need. Of course, it was no problem pressing something that small." Shelia took a few sips from the lukewarm Coca-Cola she held in her left hand.

"Wasn't Mary Fay captain of the flag team her senior year?" Charlene rummaged through the big green Naugahyde bag at her feet for the Snickers bar she'd thrown in the night before.

"I wish. No, honey, Mary Fay never did make captain, bless her heart. She was co-captain, though. Her goal since she was ten years old was to be captain of that team. But, once she turned seventeen, Mary Fay said co-captain was good enough for her. Poor thing. I always thought she sold herself short."

"Kimberly has found herself an apartment in a place called Buckhead. I wonder if an area with a name like that is a safe place for a girl to live. I guess I'm just being the overprotective mom, but I can't help worrying." Miriam looked at the veins in her hands. She hated fluorescent lighting, incandescent was so much prettier.

"That's one good thing about college. We got Donna in a sorority over in Baton Rouge, and she says it's just like home, only now she has lots of sisters. Isn't that cute? Donna always wanted sisters, had tons of dolls growing up. Her brother, Roger, was such a pain. I kind of wish God had seen fit to give me two girls. Oh, well, we can't pick our kids, now can we?" Charlene slowly shook her head and looked at Miriam.

"You can say that again. If God had let me in on the choosing, I'd of gone for one of those bookworm types. They don't sass, and they keep their rooms neat."

"I don't know," said Miriam, tearing another doughnut and returning half to the Krispy Kreme box. "I think the best traits a girl can have are good manners and nice clothes. That'll take you somewhere."

"Speaking of manners, you'd of thought the Richmonds would of had some, being such big shots and all." Shelia scratched her fingernail against the Coke can. "Do you know they told Mary Fay she'd picked out the wrong china? Don't they have gall! After the wedding, Mrs. Richmond made her take all them plates back to the jewelry store in Foley and get some fancy style she picked out. Her plates was, naturally, hand painted, and had little raised globs of paint all over'em, supposed to be flowers. They got to be washed by hand. Mary Fay says she ain't eating off nothing can't go in the dishwasher. Says it ain't sterile."

"Well, I think the biggest advantage a girl can have these days is a good education and a lot of confidence." Charlene was at the coffeepot pouring herself another cup.

"A lot of confidence? That's Mary Fay's problem; she's got too much. The girl feels like she is so accomplished at flag-waving, she don't never have to do nothing else. No sir, I think a little less self-esteem would keep a girl on her toes." Shelia pulled her third Kool from the pack.

There were two loud knocks on the closed door. All three women jumped, afraid the boss had returned early from his meeting in Atmore. An elderly lady with dyed, black hair pulled tight in a knot at the top of her head entered the smoke-filled room.

"I hate to interrupt you girls. I can see you're all busy. Shelia, there's a call for you on line three. She said it was important, but you know how Mr.Thompson feels about personal calls so you'd better make it quick," said the receptionist, trying not to inhale any smoke.

Shelia stood up with a groan and followed her to the front office. She leaned across the desk and pushed the third button on the telephone.

"Mama?" asked a timid voice on the line.

"Mary Fay, are you at home again?" Shelia glared at the receptionist who was straightening stacks of papers on her desk, pretending not to listen.

"I wasn't feeling too good today. I think it was them take-out oysters we had last night. The news had a story on about a man over in Biloxi who got hepatitis from eating oysters and died. I told you it wasn't normal to eat things that look like that."

"Mary Fay, that man had probably been carrying a sack of oysters around in the back of his pickup a week before he decided they was ripe for eating. You know how them Mississippi folks is. You gonna lose this job your Uncle Junior got for you if you keep fooling around."

"Well, I don't care. I don't like handling money nohow. It's dirty. Even when I wear those little rubber tips on my fingers, my hands turn black. You don't have no idea how many times a day I have to scrub that stuff off. It's drying my hands out and, if I use Jergen's, they just get dirtier. Anyway, I got my calling today."

"What do you mean 'calling', Mary Fay? How can you get a calling when you sitting at home all day?" Shelia's voice was getting louder and louder. The receptionist tapped a pencil on her calendar and stared at a dusty, artificial philodendron in the corner of the waiting room.

"I was watching *The Oprah Show*. It was about retired strippers who live in a nursing home down in Florida. Anyhow, the phone rang. I started not to answer it, thinking it was my boss. But it nearly rang itself to death, so I finally picked it up. I tried to talk in a hoarse whisper on account of being home and all. It was the principal at the high school. I recognized her right off – I was sent to her office enough. When she heard my muffled voice, she thought she had the wrong number and nearly hung up. I coughed and said, 'Uh, excuse me, Miss Watts, I had something lodged in my throat. I'm okay now'."

"What 'd you do, Mary Fay? Are you in trouble?"

"No, ma'am, she was calling to offer me a job. Starting in the fall, she wants me to be the sponsor of the twirl team. Well, actually, we'll begin in August. It'll be hot, but I'm used to pain. Can you believe it? It's a dream come true. All these years and finally somebody recognized my talent. They didn't forget me over at the high school. I'm a legend over there, a real legend, somebody for them girls to look up to. I knew if I was patient something like this would come along. When you give your all, other folks realize it. Sometimes it just takes 'em awhile."

"You sure do a mother proud, Baby." Shelia put the phone back in its cradle, grinned down at the receptionist and winked. "Those other girls can take their break 'til the moon turns blue. Me, I got things to do. The boss will be back pretty soon and I'm sure he'll bring piles of work. Poor thing, this place would fall apart if it weren't for me."

When summer arrived, Mary Fay's dedication became clear. She quit her job at the bank and spent June and July working on routines. Every morning, the last three weeks in August, she taught the girls synchronized marching, high-stepping, and kicking. They hated the twenty push-ups that came at the end of each day, but Mary Fay told them they had to prepare their arms for carrying the flags. It was no job for a ninety-pound weakling.

85

While sweat rolled down their faces and matted their hair, Mary Fay gave inspirational talks that kept them from giving up.

In September, the girls practiced after school everyday. If they had other activities, they had to drop them. Mary Fay told them she expected total commitment. For the first two weeks, they practiced with long sticks brought from home. When she felt everyone was ready, Mary Fay added brightly colored flags. They had to be rolled around poles, secured with ribbons, and stored in her office after practices.

Early in October, they marched in a Bay Minette parade celebrating the arts. A Pensacola television station covering the event focused on the girls wearing short smocks, waving palettes and giant paintbrushes. They did a close-up of the sponsor leading the gyrations down the street. For homecoming halftime in late October, the girls planned to wear black mini-skirts and tight, sequined tops with pointed hats and wave gold glittered brooms in the air. Mary Fay was in the middle of the football field demonstrating a dance she had seen in a movie and adapted for the show. The girls were imitating her hip swivels and pivots when her name was called from the loudspeaker over the concession stand. She ran to her office thinking something had happened to her mother at work. The call was from a publicity agent in New York City. The Pensacola station had sent him a tape, and he was impressed with the team's performance, wanted them in Macy's Thanksgiving Day Parade. The Baldwin Waves had been chosen to represent the state of Alabama.

Mary Fay called her mother and told her it would be her finest hour. Although there wasn't much time, she would put together the greatest twirling performance the world had ever seen. She and the girls would take on the awesome responsibility of representing flag wavers from across the nation.

Mary Fay designed costumes, and Shelia stayed up late nights creating halter-tops and tiny skirts from American flags donated by the American Legion. The girls would carry lit torches in the parade and dance to "America the Beautiful" as it blared from a boombox in the bed of a beribboned red, white, and blue truck trailing them. The Chevrolet dealer in Summerdale lent them a pickup with his company logo painted on both sides. He let the salesman of the month drive it to New York. Mary Fay talked the mayor into covering the team's expenses.

Everything had been so rushed, Shelia hadn't had time to worry about her daughter taking the team to a big city. After the giggling girls had tumbled out and into the airport, she pulled her church's van out of the parking lot and began to frown. None of them had been out of Baldwin County before. She hoped Mary Fay was so single-minded about their performance there would be no time for trouble.

Shelia insisted the girls from work come to her house the morning of the parade so they could watch it together. She didn't like company and hadn't had anyone over since her husband left, but she wanted to make sure they saw Mary Fay on television. She got up at daybreak and sat in the backyard, drinking cup after cup of coffee and smoking nearly a pack of cigarettes.

"Has it started yet? Did we miss anything?" asked Charlene when Shelia answered her knock on the front door. She had never been to Shelia's house and expected it to smell like a bar, cigarettes, and stale beer. Her eyes took in the room with one swipe, and she was surprised to see the curving velour sofa and matching recliner in front of the large screen TV. She had seen a couch like it on a commercial and had been begging her husband to put it on lay-away. She walked in, swinging ample hips from side to side, and placed a six-pack of Cokes, a jar of salted peanuts, and an open bag of barbeque potato chips on the oak laminated coffee table.

Miriam came in a few minutes after Charlene – she had stayed in the car to brush her hair and apply fresh lipstick – carrying a large bag of M& M's and a Tupperware box of fat-free brownies. She was going to ask Shelia how much the trip was costing the girls when one of two TV commentators sitting in a box overlooking Fifth Avenue announced the start of the parade.

The women sat down on the sofa as a giant head of Daffy Duck floated across the screen.

"Frankly, I think the cartoon characters spoil the atmosphere of this parade," said Charlene, popping the lid on a Coke.

"Honey, a parade ain't supposed to be serious," said Miriam.

Shelia sat on the edge of the sofa, hoping they didn't talk through the whole thing. She wanted to hear the perky blonde and her partner in the TV booth. She wondered if the fellow had his toupee sewn onto his scalp. It looked pretty windy there.

The first float, representing the *Nina, Pinta,* and *Santa Maria*, was led by majorettes in white cowboy outfits. The band with them was from a small town in Colorado. Shelia couldn't hear them to tell if their music was any good, but Mary Fay had told her most bands don't actually play anymore. She'd said they'd be doing good if they could even walk together.

The commentators were telling the audience how splendid the band was. They said it was too bad sound didn't carry over live television.

"It looks so breezy, maybe the notes is gone with the wind." Charlene smiled, proud of her literary reference.

Miriam opened the brownies and passed the box to Charlene and Shelia who took two each and placed them in their laps on paper napkins decorated with pastel turkeys. Miriam tore one in half and put it in her mouth.

"Look, there's the *Goodyear Blimp*," she said. "What an awful name, 'blimp'."

Donald Duck's head passed the screen in a blur. If the man in the booth hadn't told them, they wouldn't have known what it was. Streetlights were blowing at a ninety-degree angle behind him, but his hair hadn't moved. It looked like it was painted onto his head.

"That blonde shoulda worn a hat if she wanted to talk. You can't see her face for all that hair." Charlene grabbed the jar of peanuts, and they heard the shoosh as she turned the lid and air entered the bottle.

"She probably used regular hairspray instead of lacquered." Miriam patted the stiff curls at the base of her neck.

Shelia leaned closer to the television, hoping the girls would take the hint and stop talking. When a commercial was announced, she hurried outside and lit up a Kool. She couldn't hear the two inside through the sliding glass door, but knew they were talking about Mary Fay and the Waves. They stopped their conversation in mid-sentence when she came back into the room. She walked to the kitchen, filled her morning mug with coffee, and called out to see if they wanted any. Miriam took a cup with milk and two packs of Sweet n'Low. When Shelia returned to the sofa, she glanced at Charlene and saw pieces of chips around her. She thought about how the women usually left the break room. She'd have to get out the vacuum cleaner after they went home.

"You are going to miss Mary Fay if you keep smoking." Miriam leaned toward Shelia so she could smell the smoke that clung to her clothes. She missed cigarettes. She touched her stomach and remembered how thin she had been when she smoked. She wasn't sure which was worse, having lung cancer or being fat.

"It looks awfully cold there. Good thing the TV don't get too close. Otherwise the whole world would see

chill bumps on our girls. Them costumes sure is skimpy."
Charlene brushed crumbs from her lap.

The blonde on TV was holding her hair back with
her right hand and telling the audience about the exciting
group from Alabama, the Baldwin Waves. She said they
were most provocative.

"Sort of a cross between cheerleader and burlesque,
wouldn't you say, Kathy Lee?" asked the man who bent
toward her, trying to get into the camera frame. Mickey
Mouse's inflated head flapped back and forth behind them.
The big balloon seemed out of control. Below him the
Waves were wiggling their hips, tossing their lighted
torches into the air and catching them. Shelia scooted close
to the television until she sat on the floor in front of it.
Charlene and Miriam leaned left and right to see around
her.

"The atmosphere here is electric! I don't know if
it's the wind blowing or those girls and their dancing."

"This is something new at the parade, but I predict
you'll be seeing more of this type entertainment. The
crowd is going wild! You cannot hear the music, but I
believe sound is coming out of a truck following the girls."

Mickey was flying low and starting to bounce from
building to building as spectators ducked and covered their
heads. He was tugging on a rope attached to a small

platform that slid along the street in front of Mary Fay. As he twisted free, she jumped forward and grabbed the end of the dangling rope in her left hand, still clutching the torch in her right. She was lifted above the girls who continued their routine as if nothing was happening. She looked down at them and smiled, remembering teaching them that the show must go on, no matter what.

A gust of wind blew Mickey over the girls and above the float that came next, "The Thanksgiving Feast." It was made from California roses and had living Pilgrims and Indians sitting down together in peace. John Smith sat with Pocahontas, and William Bradford shared a pipe with an old chief in a colorful, feathered headpiece. A giant white pedestal rose from the center of the table and was crowned with a cornucopia of fruit and vegetables.

Mary Fay could see a group of schoolchildren jumping up and down, clapping and laughing as the balloon swerved in their direction. Mickey was diving right into the kids. Mary Fay did a pirouette on the rope and tossed her flaming torch into the air. It did a triple flip and landed precisely where she intended, in Mickey's left nostril.

The balloon exploded and plastic bits fell from the sky like confetti. Mary Fay's skirt flew up and all the crowed could see were long legs topped by starred bikini panties as she landed in a perfect split atop a flowered pineapple in the cornucopia.

The camera flashed back to the announcers who were almost too shaken to speak. "That brave woman just saved the lives of hundreds, mostly children. The crowd here is in awe of her bravery. They won't stop cheering."

"Kathy Lee, miraculously, she seems unhurt. She is shimmying down the pedestal and the Pilgrims and Indians are helping her off the float. Wait, I just got word that the mayor is running through the crowd toward her. He plans to offer her the key to the city."

"Wasn't Pope John the last one to receive it?"

"That's right, Kathy Lee. Maybe this girl will be canonized."

"Well, there's no doubt in anybody's mind that we have all witnessed a miracle here today."

Shelia spun around and looked at the two open-mouthed women sitting on the edge of her sofa. "What did you say your daughters were doing?"

RIDING THE WAVES

Amelia wondered what she was doing in a
psychiatrist's office. She should never have listened to
Elaine at work. She hadn't fallen for any of her schemes
before and thought she must be getting weak or senile to
think this was a good idea. Elaine talked so much maybe
she needed to pay someone to listen. She was just the type
to think blabbing to somebody else would make her
troubles go away. It was Elaine's changed behavior that
had really gotten to Amelia. She had gone from Lucrezia
to Pollyanna since she started taking Prozac. It hadn't had
that effect on Amelia. In the two months she'd been on it,
all she noticed was that her sex drive – what was left of it –
was gone. She didn't want to be Suzy Sunshine anyway.
She was much too intelligent to ignore reality. Amelia
didn't understand why she had to come to this dreary office
once a week. Didn't the doctor or at least his cheery
receptionist know gray walls were depressing? And why
the Edward Hopper prints? She smiled at the idea of
patients sitting in the leather chairs under the gilt framed

pictures. They were as empty as Hopper's buildings. The receptionist glanced up from her schedule book, like she did every few minutes, and gave Amelia a smile between pink lips penciled in dark brown. Amelia imagined an egg timer going off at appointed minutes. Maybe her cheerfulness kept some patients from going over the edge.

When the doctor came out of his booklined office to greet her, she allowed herself to be led down the small hallway and into his territory again. Amelia was careful not to let him know how much she hated these visits. She was cordial, answered his question about how her week had been and even asked about his, not that she was interested. He told her they were there to make sure she felt good; he didn't matter in this situation. She thought she'd feel better if she could get out of the cramped office and away from the dry smell of Kleenex. She wanted to feel better but didn't see how this was going to help. She felt like she was being interrogated at police headquarters. And she didn't like the way he stopped her in mid sentence when her forty-five minutes was up. Something in her Puritan upbringing rebelled against paying for a full hour and only getting three-fourths. But she kept her disappointment to herself, a skill she had long ago mastered, and didn't let the doctor know what was really bothering her. Amelia was boiling like a volcano inside.

Amelia's brother, Michael, had killed himself four years earlier. He was her favorite brother, and there were plenty to choose from, five in all. She had been the only girl in the family. Now everybody had excuses for falling out of touch, the way families do. They had tried to get together a few times at Christmas or Easter, but, they all really preferred to celebrate at their own homes. Even though Michael was the only one, besides her, who still lived in New Orleans, she hadn't seen him for years before he died. Amelia's husband, Tom, didn't like Michael, called him a loser. He said Michael talked too much and complained about his problems instead of being a man and handling them like everybody else. The last time Amelia had Michael over to dinner was in 1990, his birthday, New Year's Day.

The kids had enjoyed his visit and she had, too. Catching up on old times was almost like having them again. Michael seemed better than she had expected. He was glad to see her and get to know her family. And he certainly was in need of a good meal; he was thin as a rail. But, then, as children, the two of them had been the skinny ones, full of energy. Later, when she and Tom went to bed, Tom said he hoped they never had to endure that sniveling bore in their house again. He said that Michael was in the bathroom half the night doing coke, and that he could tell by the way Michael slurred his speech that he was drunk on top of that. Amelia noticed that Tom was slurring a little when he told her this. It must have been the four bottles of merlot the three of them had consumed before, during, and after dinner. Tom warned her not to have her brother over again, and she had intended to do it anyway, just to spite Tom, but she never found the time.

Michael was found, two days after his death, in a flophouse off Camp Street. He had taken a whole bottle of Percodans and had drunk most of a bottle of some rotgut whiskey. Now, Amelia was on pills herself. And she and Tom had started drinking more and more. She remembered when they started dating that she wasn't much of a drinker, but Tom had insisted that a little was good, "to take the edge off". Now it was the only thing that made conversation bearable between them. She knew he felt the same way. They had started with a bottle at dinner every night, after the kids were put to bed. Now it had escalated to two bottles most nights and sometimes three. Amelia found herself waking up most mornings with an empty wineglass on her nightstand beside her pillow. Having a drink with dinner was continental – waking up with a wineglass was strictly American.

When Amelia's mother left messages, Amelia found she didn't have time to call her back. How had her mother raised so many children? Well, times were different then. Maids were reliable and wanted the work; they needed the work. She had to hire a Honduran to keep her kids. Thank God she had taken Spanish in school, even minored in it. Of course, she probably wouldn't have if it hadn't been for her friend Ella, from Panama. They had big plans to represent their countries in those days. Ella wanted to get involved in international politics back in Panama, and Amelia wanted to become a diplomat, a go-between for the United States and some Latin country. Now Ella was an English teacher in an American college in Panama, and Amelia had never even visited a foreign country, although she and Tom had talked about traveling often enough. They were saving money for the children's education. The kids deserved the best schools money could buy, and no matter what it took to get them, that's what would be done. She was willing to sacrifice. And even if there was enough money, there wasn't enough time to waste on trips.

The boys were becoming good chess players and were on the school team. They were fortunate to have a good chess coach. How many children got the chance to study under an international chess player? Chess was a game Amelia had long wanted to learn. She had meant to keep up with the kids, but they had surpassed her limited skills long ago, and no one wanted to play with her now.

Tommy was becoming a soccer star at school. He had inherited his father's natural athletic abilities and competitiveness. He wanted to be a sports attorney when he grew up. That would make all the trips to the soccer field worth it. Amelia just wished there was a field closer to their house so that she had time to stop and watch a game every now and then. She took the baby to her ballet and gymnastics classes on the same days Tommy practiced and had games, so she missed watching him play. It would be nice if the dance studio were a little closer to the soccer field.

Carl didn't like soccer as much as his big brother; he was not a competitive child, and he didn't like the idea of following in Tommy's footsteps. He preferred sailing and horseback riding, and he played the trumpet. Amelia knew that, when the kids were grown, the skills they learned early would get them into finer circles. Her job was to make sure all three of them got a solid base and learned as many things as they could. They could decide later which ones they wanted to stick with. Like a hostess at a party, Amelia was there simply to make the introductions. The relationships could develop as they might – that was not the job of the hostess. She often felt like she was arranging a party for someone else, setting things up, seeing that everyone had a good time, that things went well, and cleaning up afterwards. The problem was, she was not enjoying the party.

Her analyst had suggested she take a few weeks off and maybe even take a little trip, go somewhere by herself. Didn't he know her family depended on her? The analyst was getting on her nerves, and she couldn't see any improvement. If there was one thing she couldn't afford right now it was to waste her time. She was thinking about quitting. She tried to make it clear, without being rude, that this was way off base, but the psychiatrist was starting to make her talk about Michael anyway. He even suggested that Michael had been manic-depressive and that the disorder ran in families. He said Lithium probably would have helped Michael. She was not even considering taking it, if that was what he was getting at. Prozac was a pop cure, but Lithium was a whole other ballgame. One of her cousins was a zombie on the stuff.

Her doctor wanted to know how her father died. She guessed the local medical profession had speculated on his death because he'd been a doctor. There was the hint of suicide, but he had to take medication for his hip. Her father was in constant pain from an old football injury.

That's why he sometimes pulled Michael and John from their beds and beat them. Amelia had awakened to fights on the hall steps between her brothers and their father on more than one occasion. At these times, their mother hid herself in Amelia's room, too frightened for her own safety to help her children. He never bothered the other children. He said that Michael and John looked just like their mother, and the other boys looked like him. Amelia wondered whom she looked like. The morning after such fights, their father would go off on his rounds as if nothing had happened, leaving his family in shambles.

Maybe, she thought, there was something wrong with Daddy that made him act that way and, maybe, Michael had inherited it. But, she hadn't – definitely not. She was a success in high school and college, had a promising career, a gorgeous husband, and three great kids. There was nothing wrong with her. She just needed more time. If she didn't have the damn sessions once a week, she could start swimming again. They paid outrageous fees to belong to the country club. There were two great pools there, one with Olympic sized laps. She used to love swimming, and it was bound to be stress relieving as well as good exercise. She sure didn't need to lose any weight, though. Amelia had seen her old friend, Lesley, at the grocery store and had barely recognized her. She had really let herself go; she looked matronly. Amelia hoped that never happened to her. Her weight was exactly what it had been in college. She wondered how many of her class mates could say that. Lately, however, she looked thinner than she actually was. Maybe her mother was right. Maybe women over forty needed a little padding to plump out the wrinkles.

Amelia didn't eat much anymore. At night, she and Tom ate later and later, and sometimes it was so late, she was too tired to eat. What she really wanted to do was drink. It was the only thing she still enjoyed. Wine relaxed her and it had become her friend, keeping the loneliness away. If she could just have a glass of chardonnay while he ate, Tom could chat and chat about his daily activities. She would nod and agree and make perfectly placed comments. She had mastered the routine both during dinner and afterwards. She would appear to be present when, in actuality, her mind was a million miles away, at rest from her hectic day. When Tom was satisfied with his own conversation, he would go upstairs to their room, take a Tylenol P.M., and slip into bed. This was Amelia's favorite time, when she had the world to herself. She often sat in the backyard, in the iron chair beside the barbecue pit they hadn't used since the first year they had moved into the house. Amelia was glad her body did not require much sleep and that she could enjoy the nighttime. The neighbor's dog stopped his constant yelping, the birds and the insects went to sleep. Even the mosquitoes went to sleep at night. Tom liked to sit in the backyard at sunset, but she was cooking the kids' supper then, and anyway, at sunset, the mosquitoes feasted on her like tiny kings at a banquet. Tom said they naturally went to people who ate a lot of sweets, but she didn't really eat any. She couldn't understand their need to drain her blood. They were just like everybody else, trying to suck the life out of her.

Dr. Cyr, the psychiatrist, was the same way. Amelia could tell that he was becoming interested in her. She had heard of the phenomenon. Weak patient falls into the strong arms of powerful physician. He was the needy one in the relationship. What kind of person makes his living listening to the private sufferings of other people? All psychiatrists were crazy, or they wouldn't be in that business. Didn't they have a high rate of suicide? Like dentists, they should have been real doctors. If they were so smart, why didn't they ever fix anybody? Why wasn't Dr. Cyr a brain surgeon? Amelia was going to have to stop wasting her time. Time was the problem and why should she give her most precious commodity to a stranger and pay him to insult her? She was in a rut. That was why she had hired a psychiatrist in the first place, to help her get back on her feet. He could go ahead and cure her, help her with time management, or he could find himself another sucker. Shrinks were as common in New Orleans as lawyers. Just because he was a man, he thought things could be black and white. She should have hired a female doctor. She didn't know what had come over her to see a psychiatrist anyway. All she did was go in, sit down, clock faced away from her, discreetly but as a silent reminder of the doctor's valuable time, and run her mouth...blah, blah, blah. He asked a few well-toned questions, like, "How does that make you feel? How do you feel about that? What were your feelings when..." They were questions any reasonably bright person could answer without giving anything away.

The doctor had given her a book on time management. She told him she hadn't been able to find the time to read in a life too short on time. He had intimated that if she wanted to feel better and to be able to better manage her time, she would need to address certain issues in her life. Actually, she had read a little of the book during her lunch breaks. It was just another of the millions of self-help books flooding the market of the current narcissistic society. She felt she'd be just as well off reading a book written by a television talk show host on the meaning of life and the universe. He just didn't get it.

People with time problems had no time to read books about time.

Amelia decided to make some changes. After Tom finished dinner and went up to bed, she had her last glass of wine in the backyard. She went into the kitchen and took her keys out of the drawer under the telephone and picked up her purse from the countertop. She stepped out of the sleeping house and onto the front stoop. Stopping to pet each of the two striped yellow cats waiting by the door, she made her way past the blue water delivery bottles. She smiled to herself at the thought that she would no longer have to fuss at Tom to carry them into the house. She always ended up dragging them in herself anyway.

The station wagon was waiting in the driveway like a boat at the dock. Before they became yuppie cars, Volvos were considered the intelligent choice among car owners. Everybody in Massachusetts drove one when she was there for college, and she had insisted that she and Tom buy one for their first car. He had been sold on them ever since. Now she wondered if they were really worth the extra cost and repairs. She would be just as happy driving an American car. The purpose of a vehicle was to run errands anyway. Driving hadn't been fun for a long time.

Before Amelia put the keys in the ignition, she took the house key and the key to her office off the key chain and dropped them on the shell driveway beside the car. After backing out and away from her house, Amelia reached for the radio dial and set it for the late night blues program she enjoyed. She was glad the boys weren't in the car to fight over the station. She usually didn't allow the radio to be turned on because of their arguing over it. As she started going down the main street that led to the highway, Amelia began to relax and her mind to drift. It wasn't long before she was singing along with Billie Holiday. Next was a taped interview with a local blues singer from the Quarter who was making it big. He said the blues had saved his life. Amelia thought to herself that the blues were her life. And she sang along with him when he performed "I Ain't Got Nothin' but the Blues". She thought maybe the heat and the thickness of the air in New Orleans helped to create the blues and that all New Orleanians suffered from it. She was glad to be going and leaving it all behind. What she needed was space and fresh air. Westerners lived out in the open, without all the Spanish moss draping over everything and choking out life. You didn't hear of anyone out West singing the blues. But there was a lot between New Orleans and the West, a lot of swamp and miles and miles of interstate. She wanted to get somewhere fast, and when she had the choice to go left or right on I10, she headed east, to the Gulf of Mexico.

Amelia's mother had a cousin in Alabama. Every summer she used to invite Amelia to their beach house in Gulf Shores so Amelia could play with her daughters, Sally and Maida. They stayed at the beach all summer, and Amelia spent July with them. They were chocolate colored by the time she arrived and her tan never caught up to theirs. All three of them had white eyelids in their dark faces because their eyes were always open. They were busy little girls, building sandcastles, chasing crabs on the beach, and riding the waves. Amelia never learned to ride as effortlessly as the Alabama cousins. They could have been in the Olympics if there had been a wave-riding category. They said it was all in the rhythm. Every fourth wave was the one to catch, the three before it were merely builders. A body has to get out in the water, thigh deep, and get into the motion of the waves, to wait for the good ones, and not waste energy on the little waves that lacked the power to carry you all the way to the beach. You had to catch the wave just as it was breaking, not before and not after, because that is the point at which each wave has the most force. The girls could turn within the waves, adjusting the direction in which they were thrown, and when they rode, their thin, dark bodies were like torpedoes shot straight to the beaches of Normandy. Now, Maida was an architect in Atlanta and Amelia had lost touch with her. Sally was a housewife raising a family in Montgomery. She was good about sending Christmas cards with her children's pictures on them so Amelia could pretend that she knew them. She wondered if Sally had taught them the fine art of wave riding.

Amelia was getting close to the Mississippi coast and she decided to get off the interstate and drive along the beach. The casinos had changed the area even more than Hurricane Camille. She had no idea there were so many. When had gambling become America's favorite pastime? And when had gambling become a family activity? The casinos were miniature Disney Worlds moored to the docks. Unlike the sleaze she had associated with gambling, these places were giant playgrounds of neon lights. Something about their pretense of fun and promise was even dirtier to her than the Las Vegas of old. But the casinos were packing in the customers. Even though it must have been nearly three-thirty in the morning, the parking lots were filled with car tags from all over the southeast.

Amelia thought she should stop for coffee because she still had a long way to go if she was to make it to the Gulf and her cousins' old house. She knew it was still there because Sally had mentioned it on some of her cards. She just hoped it was like she remembered it and not redone, condominium style. She loved the old, dark, pine walls and the sleeping porch her cousins had shared with her. Their mother didn't seem to mind that there was sand everywhere, even in the sheets. She said sand was just something you lived with at the beach. Amelia wondered if they had air conditioned the whole house or still had only the window unit in the parents' bedroom. She thought about her aunt's cold drip coffee and how she would fix it in the mornings for the girls with more than half the cup of milk and sugar. They called it coffee-milk and felt very grown-up drinking it from fancy cups with matching saucers. This morning Amelia would settle for a mug at The Waffle House.

When she pulled into the restaurant, she noticed only one car in the parking lot, a dirty and battered Pontiac from Georgia. As she stepped inside, the waitress yelled out the prerequisite "Good Morning!" Amelia wondered to herself what the management had been thinking when they decided to make this a part of the service. It all but made her turn around and walk right back out. But, she did need to stop and drink some coffee, even if acting phony was part of the deal. Sitting at a booth was a couple who were in their late sixties or early seventies. The man looked like a bad imitation of Elvis in his later years – years he failed to reach. The woman had hair that had been dyed red so long ago it was turning pink, and her face was heavily made up. It was difficult to say which of the two was wearing more jewelry; they were both wrapped in gold chains and studded rings. They were whispering together and smoking Camel Lights. The ashtray was overflowing with ashes and butts. Somehow, the woman looked even worse smoking than the man. Amelia remembered how, when she was a child, the men had openly enjoyed cigarettes, but the women had hidden to do their smoking. Her bathroom always smelled like smoke because that's where her mother hid to indulge. She was glad that she never started. It would be another habit to give up in the middle years. She attributed her never starting smoking to her grandmother who said you must never pick up two things, cigarettes and men, because you'll never be able to put them down again. Amelia sat at the counter, ordered coffee, and drank it straight. It made her shudder a little because it was so strong. She wondered how long it had been sitting in the metal canister.

After the coffee, Amelia stopped at an all night BP gas station, filled up the car, and used the bathroom. Then she was back on the interstate and heading for Mobile. The highway could have been anywhere USA – they all looked the same and so did the exits. Life was becoming homogenized in this country. Pretty soon, she thought, we'll all be clones just like our environments. She passed a sign that read "Welcome to Alabama the Beautiful" and thought that it looked just like "Mississippi, the Magnolia State." From the interstate, they were the same. A person could travel across the entire country on the interstate and hardly realize he had left home.

Before she knew it, Amelia was on the Bayway and crossing Mobile Bay. The sun was coming up in front of her eyes in a profusion of pastels. It looked like a parasol spinning in a soft sky. The brown water of the bay became iridescent silver, and she felt like she was gliding across its surface. Thoughts of her life were gone, and she was like one of the pelicans skimming the water in a long and sweeping line, a part of a graceful whip of action. Amelia was going home to a place she hadn't known in a long time, a place of quiet and calm.

Gulf Shores was bigger than she remembered. She stopped at a convenience store that was just opening up and purchased a plastic raft. There were only two in the bin outside the store, and she took the aqua one decorated with seashells. Fort Morgan Road seemed shorter than it used to, and she was at her cousins' house before she knew it. The old yellow house looked smaller but the same, untouched by the ravages of modern decoration. She went straight to the beach and began taking off her clothes. She threw them on the sand and walked to the water's edge. The water was chilly and she thought about her cousins saying only Yankees got in the water when it wasn't summer. But October had been mild, they were experiencing Indian summer, so she thought the cousins would approve if she went in. The water was cold, and she knew the only way to deal with the shock of it was to dive in and get her body used to the temperature. The waves were big and she dove straight into one. The water churned above her head but she was in the smoother part near the bottom of the turbulence. Amelia came through the water to the other side and was rewarded with a slap in the face from the wave coming next. These were just the kinds of waves that her cousins loved, but they were too strong for her. After diving into a few more, so as not to get knocked down by their force, Amelia caught a ride on one to the beach. It was faster than she had anticipated, and it ground her nose into the sand as it threw her onto drier land.

Back on the beach, Amelia lay on her raft to catch her breath, but as soon as she relaxed, she began to sweat. As the sweat trickled off her body onto the raft, she began to get uncomfortable. The sun was hotter now and her skin was starting to stick to the raft. There was nothing to do but go back in the water. She grabbed a corner of the raft and pulled it behind her into the surf. The waves began a tug-of-war with her for the raft. If she held the raft in front of her, she got hit in the face with it, and if she carried it behind, the waves caught it and pulled her down. She had to carry it overhead and push her way through. It took her a little while, but she made it past the breakers to the calmer water. It was soon over her head, and she climbed up on the raft, her island in the middle of the Gulf. There had been a sandbar out past the breakers when they were children. They used to go there and dive for sand dollars. When they found a lot of them, they took them home and dried them out for days. They coated the shells with Elmer's Glue to make them hard and keep them white. One year they found enough for the cousins to cover their entire Christmas tree with them instead of ornaments. Sally said it was beautiful but that the top was bare because they had been unable to find a starfish. Amelia put her arms over the sides of the raft and began paddling out into the deeper water. She pulled with her arms until they were sore from rubbing the sides of the raft. She turned around and realized she could no longer see the clump of wrinkled clothes she had left on the beach. In fact, she couldn't make out anything on the shore, just a fading white line at the water's edge. She thought about what a good floater she had been as a kid. None of her brothers could stay up, but she could go for what seemed hours on her back, looking up at the clouds. She put her arms behind her head, elbows out, and remembered floating. And she thought about Mexico.

LOCATIONS

Ellen didn't know what to expect when her husband's law firm transferred them to Mobile. They came from Germantown, outside Memphis, where she raised horses and taught children to ride. She'd never thought of Mobile, didn't know anything about it except that the natives laid claim to the birth of Mardi Gras, a frivolous honor, she thought. The firm rented a house for them on a small lot along a winding, narrow lane in Springhill. There were so many large houses close together that the street reminded her of Fraternity Row at college. They'd been in Mobile about three months when I met her. Our daughters sat next to each other in Miss Hixon's second grade and became friends the first day of school.

My little girl, Susan, wanted Ellen's daughter, Rebecca, to spend the night at our house. I like to know my child's friends' parents, so I called Ellen and invited her to meet me at the local coffee shop. I got there early so I could do some work for a graduate class at the university. I was reading an essay on Southern literature when she walked into the café. A sea of Mobile matrons flooded the place, and she stuck out like red at a funeral. She had short, loose, black curls and wore a floppy hat, a cloth dahlia pinned to the front. Her oversized black dress and purple vest would have appeared silly on most small women, but looked elegant on her. I stood up and walked over, introduced myself, and led her to my table beneath a window. She glanced at my open book and said she didn't know anyone read anything other than self-help anymore. When the waitress came, she ordered cappuccino and I, black coffee.

I asked about art shows in Memphis, and she told me she had been an active board member at the museum. The only time I had been there was for the King Tut exhibit years before. She said she enjoyed art, but what she missed were her horses. She had kept eight on their property and had planned to bring two to Mobile as soon as she found a barn that boarded.

Her husband, Jack, had moved to Mobile in the spring, but Ellen waited for Rebecca's school to be out for the summer. One May morning she loaded hay bales into the pickup and carried them to the pasture. The horses usually raced toward the truck for their feed, but that day none came. Two horses, a bay mare and a chestnut gelding, were lying on their sides and refused to get up even when she slapped their rumps and pulled their manes.

117

Ellen went back to the house as fast as she could drive and called the vet who came within the hour. He said there was a deadly disease going around that had killed several horses in Tennessee. No vaccine had been developed for it, and contagious animals had to be shot before it spread. He was surprised she hadn't heard about it, but Ellen didn't read newspapers and wouldn't allow television in the house. She didn't listen to a radio although many trainers kept one going in the stables to calm their horses. She played tapes of classical music. She wasn't sure some of it, like Wagner, made them less nervous, but she believed it made them more intelligent. After the vet left, she lay on the ground beside the horses, patting them and talking, until the school bus arrived bringing her daughter home from school. She and Rebecca sat with the dying animals until late that night hoping for recovery.

Although the vet had offered, she couldn't let a stranger shoot her horses. She knew she would have to do it. The next morning, she put her husband's Winchester 338 in the back of the truck and drove to the bahia field. The same two horses were on the ground as was Cadillac, her favorite.

Ellen's husband had surprised her with the mare the year they purchased the property. She was the first horse Ellen had ridden since she was a girl. When the horse trader had brought the horse to their place, Ellen had ridden her around the pasture once, trotting so smoothly posting wasn't necessary. She had never ridden an animal with such a smooth gait.

The horse dealer said, "Ma'am, she may be little, but what she lacks in size, she makes up for in style. She's a Cadillac." The name had stuck.

Ellen's breath became shallow when she saw Cadillac lying near the white fence at the back of the pasture.

She drove to the middle of the field, turned off the engine, took a deep breath and got out, leaving the door ajar. She reached into the bed of the truck, picked up the gun, and walked toward the two horses. She shot the female first and then the male. They lay still, waiting for the bullets. They were too weak to lift their heads and never opened their eyes. Ellen got back into the cab, hands shaking, and drove, never leaving first gear, to Cadillac. She stopped and stepped out of the truck, leaving the motor running, and moved slowly toward the animal who lay in the grass before her, its skin damp with dew. Cadillac turned her head sideways and looked at her with one velvet brown eye as Ellen lifted the gun to her shoulder and pulled back the cold steel hammer. The rifle jerked upward when the bullet left the chamber, and Ellen was thrown two steps back as the hot metal landed in the animal's flesh with a thud. Thick purple blood drained from the hole in Cadillac's right flank as the horse continued to stare, rocking its body forward, going first to bent knees and then back, before standing, like a colt rising for the first time, on wobbly legs. Cadillac looked like a drunk determined to keep her balance as she careened toward Ellen, swaying from side to side. Ellen heard the vet's words in her head, "You'll know an animal has the disease because it will be impossible for him to stand." She realized Cadillac had just been sleeping. As the horse moved toward her, a questioning but trusting look in its eyes, Ellen lifted the gun, aimed, and fired, this time into the heart.

The following month she sold the five other horses and cleared out the barn.

Ellen was looking out the window as expensive, four wheel drive vehicles filed past on the street, identical except in color, like cars in a showroom. I sat across from her, my hand around the cold cup, the coffee long since gone. In my attention to the story, I had drunk too fast and burned the tip of my tongue and it tingled. Most people have an easy time opening up to me, so I am burdened with their secrets. This woman, whom I had known for an hour, had been talking as fast as an auctioneer, like she hadn't spoken with anyone for years.

We started meeting at the coffee shop every Wednesday morning and she told me more and more about her life. She had hoped the move to Mobile would keep her husband home, but he was away on business twice as much as before, mostly to New Orleans, and she was lonely. She thought she would have more friends and more to do if they moved elsewhere. She didn't like living in a town where women were named Sugie, Pixie, and Bama. She said they were cheerleaders from the moment of conception. She said women with names like that needed to marry rich and stay young. The ones she met belonged to social organizations called The Belles, The Maenads, and The MAM's. They dressed in expensive suits with matching purses and shoes for meetings at the country club and got floor-scrubbing drunk and screwed each other's husbands at Mardi Gras balls. Ellen knew she wasn't missing anything by being left out, but resented the exclusion.

She came from high society in Tennessee. Her mother was a socialite and had been Queen of the Cotton Carnival, the top of the ladder in Memphis. It was a throne her mother started walking toward when Ellen was a baby. She had divorced Ellen's father, a sweet, country man from Chattanooga, and married Buddy Gerrard, a millionaire who could afford to make her dreams come true. Buddy had inherited his father's company, and it ran itself while he played cards and drank whiskey with the boys in the back room at the club. Ellen's mother and Buddy didn't have any children together, and she grew up alone in their Tudor mansion. Her friend was her horse, Bella, and they rode every afternoon in the fields surrounding the house. When Ellen left Memphis for the university, she wanted to take Bella but Buddy wouldn't hear of it, said he was sending a girl, not a horse, to get an education. When she came home for Christmas, the first place she went was the barn. Bella was gone. Buddy had gotten rid of her the second week Ellen had left.

For as long as she could remember, Ellen had hated Buddy's kisses. Other grown-ups kissed her cheek, not mouth. Her mother said she was lucky to be so loved. He liked Ellen to sit on his lap so he could rub her back with stiff, claw-like fingers, up and down, up and down, as her muscles tightened. When she was fifteen and her mother had flown to New York with friends for a shopping spree, Buddy took Ellen to the country club for dinner. The two of them had never been out, but he said she would be dating soon and needed to learn how to act. They stayed a long time at the club, going to the bar after the meal so Buddy could talk with friends and have more drinks. On the drive back, he placed his hand on her knee and asked if she thought much about boys. He wanted to know if she was curious about dating. Ellen told him the boys at school acted dumb, and she wasn't interested in them. She was uncomfortable and stared out the window. His hand had moved to her thigh. She wished he'd let her spend the night at her friend's house.

She thought they'd never get home. Buddy was driving slower than usual and weaving across the yellow line. Ellen tried to race upstairs as soon as he opened the back door, but Buddy told her to come into the den to talk. He patted the sofa beside him. Ellen looked around as if checking exits, sighed, and sat on the damask cushions. Buddy told her to lie down for a backrub. She thought about running out of the room but was afraid to disobey him. He told her to loosen up as his rough hands raked back and forth across her tense back.

"Roll over," he said. She did, staring at the ceiling so she wouldn't have to see his face. "You look just like your mother tonight." Ellen tried to hold her breath so as not to smell the sickeningly sweet sour mash odor mingled with his usual halitosis. His hands slid from right shoulder to left, pushing down the scooped neckline of her dress and exposing the top of her bra. Ellen's body froze, and she thought about the first time she had been introduced to Buddy. When they shook hands, his fat, untapered fingers wrapped around hers like he was smothering a bird.

Now, one of his hands rested like an iron weight on her collarbone while the other slid down between her breasts and back to her throat. She held up her palms and pushed against his chest. He grabbed both wrists and jerked down her arms. Her right hand snagged on a pencil sticking out of is pocket and the lead broke off and dug deep into the skin. He let go for a second, looking at the yellow stub, and she scooted to the opposite end of the sofa, pulled herself up, and slid off. Buddy chuckled and straightened to a sitting position. Ellen ran upstairs and locked her bedroom door as he picked the remote off the coffee table and flicked on the television.

Leaning across the table, Ellen pushed aside her half-empty cup, opened her right hand, and pointed with a wooden coffee stirrer to the gray pencil point lodged deep in her palm. It was a part of her now.

She told me her mother and stepfather had been leaving a fundraiser for the Catholic hospital when they hit an eighteen-wheeler bound for Amarillo. They were killed instantly, and although he had pulled out in front of the truck, no one in Memphis ever admitted that Buddy had been drunk. Ellen took the front page of an old newspaper from a lavender suede bag she had hung on the back of her chair when she arrived at the coffee shop. She placed it on the table between us, and I read the headlines, "Memphis Loses Buddy." It was an article about the kindness and generosity of her stepfather, a man she said was so stingy at home he once stole coins from atop her dresser to teach her a lesson not to leave money lying around.

As the months passed, my daughter and Ellen's spent every evening on the phone talking and weekends together at our house or theirs. Ellen and I spent more time together, taking the girls shopping, out to dinner, and to movies. She was an early riser and called me almost every morning around six. The closer we seemed to get, the farther away I felt. I was uncomfortable around her because I felt she was desperate for friendship. I don't like feeling sorry for people but took her on almost as a hobby, something to fix. Her husband was away more than he was home. She said they didn't talk anyway; he was consumed by work. I only met him once, at a dinner Ellen gave to celebrate his promotion. I was seated beside him and tried to engage him in conversation. He had a dull look in his eyes until he told me about a case he was handling for an international company. It was the only time he looked at me all evening, and I felt like I was sitting next to an empty chair.

To give Ellen something to do, Jack rented an empty beach house she could decorate at Dauphin Island. He had never seen it, but she had been going there every weekend, when, in April, she invited Susan and me down for a night.

Around noon, Saturday, my daughter and I drove the fifteen miles to the island. We saw monstrous pilings rising from the brown water of Mobile Bay as we neared the bridge. Slender strips of sand, home to turtles, fiddler crabs, and seabirds, lay like scarves tossed across the water. Just before our ascent to the paved mountain, we saw flat oysters boats gently rocking in the murky backwater hammocks running to the bay. Beige reeds and pale green bamboo swayed on the bank beside them. At daybreak, thin, weathered oystermen would return, motor out, and with long, metal tongs, yank cement-like clusters from the water's sandy bottom. After boarding the island, we took a right at the main intersection and drove west on the road dividing the land into gulfside and bayside. Dauphin Island is a place of longleaf pines and scrub oaks where wooden houses perch on stilts like cranes at the water's edge. Susan spotted Rebecca waving from the landing at the top of the stairs leading to Ellen's yellow house.

After unloading our suitcases, Ellen, the girls, and I toured the brick Confederate fort and looked for nests at the bird sanctuary in the dunes. We had lunch at a hamburger stand, and the girls drank milkshakes while we had a few beers. Afterward, Ellen drove us to the liquor store, and she came out with three bottles of wine. In the afternoon we sat in the sand in front of her house, and she kept wineglasses filled while our daughters built sandcastles on the beach. All four of us clapped as the sun fell into the Gulf, leaving vivid red and orange streaks across strips of sinewy clouds. I was thinking of the green flash said to follow the sun in certain climates when Ellen told me every sunset made her contemplate mortality. We watched the light slowly fade away while the girls gathered driftwood and built a bonfire. We roasted hotdogs on straightened coat hangers and charred marshmallows until they were crusts of crisp black around steaming, creamy lumps.

Our sunburned children went to bed early, whispering for about thirty minutes before sleep found them in the iron bunks of the back bedroom. Ellen and I sat creaking in white wicker rockers on the screened porch, watching the stars. Above dark waves fringed with white lace, the blackness of the sky was interrupted by dots of light piercing its surface. It had been years since I had seen the shadowy tunnel of the Milky Way. Ellen and I sat and rocked, as if waiting for something to fall out of the Big Dipper. She said she found peace near the water; it was the only time she could be herself. She told me she was grateful I was her confidante, someone she could trust. I continued rocking and hoped she didn't notice my silence. The alcohol magnified my guilt and I wanted to shout that if it were not for my daughter, I would not be her friend. I found her needy personality repugnant, and was afraid if I spent much more time with her, she would suck the life out of me.

I stood up and stumbled into the hall and to the front bedroom I was to use. It was dark and I bumped my shin on a wooden trunk at the foot of the bed. I did not want to disturb the quietness of the night with the blare of light, so I held out my hands and felt my way along the wall to the bathroom door. I remembered the layout from the afternoon and found my way to the toilet and then the sink. When I came out I heard breathing and, in the bluish light of the moon, saw Ellen leaning against the side of the mattress. I wondered why she was there because her room and bath were across the hall. Her presence made me uncomfortable, like someone's handwriting among your notes. I could feel her eyes on me, but I didn't know what to say. I was dizzy from the wine and having trouble keeping my balance.

"Come here," she said and reached toward me, tugging at my wrist. I moved next to her, placing my hip beside the bed to steady myself. She grasped my upper arms and pulled me closer. Her voice was devoid of emotion and I wondered what her expression might be. Shadows hid her face, the moonlight coming through the window behind her. I could see the circle of dark curls around her head and thought how inappropriate it was for a solemn person to have lively hair. A part down the middle of long, straight strands would better suit her. Her clothes were cheerful, too, and didn't seem to match her moods. This night she wore billowy silk pants and a Hawaiian print shirt.

She put her arms around my waist and across my back. I placed my fingers on the thin blades of her shoulders and felt the bone barely covered with skin. It was as if there was nothing holding her up, and I was afraid she would drop to the floor in a broken pile. Her body reminded me of my great-aunt when I helped the nurse lift her from bed to wheelchair. She was without substance, like a down pillow.

Bending toward me, Ellen said, "Kiss me." She put her mouth on mine in such a confident manner I knew it wasn't the first time she had been with a woman. My lips trembled, and I thought of playing spin-the-bottle in the

129

sixth grade. Those boys were nice to kiss; their beardless faces didn't prick your skin like a man's shaved one. The inside of her mouth was no different from a man's, and I realized that behind lips, as in the heart, men and women are the same. I found her next kiss sexually arousing until I began to fear she would touch my body. An involuntary shudder passed through me, and I recalled a man I once stopped dating because his hands were smooth and smaller than mine. I felt like I couldn't breathe with her soft breasts pressed against mine, and I remembered the rise and fall of my ex-husband's hard chest as he breathed and the safety I felt resting my head on his shoulders.

"This is too weird for me," I said, pulling away from the bed. My head was spinning from the wine, and I pushed my hand against the wall for support.

She let her arms fall with a heavy drop, straightened her back and pushed her hair from the sides of her face. Without a word she walked out. The air was still, and I heard her close the door to her bedroom.

I lay between cotton sheets on the bed and listened to the Gulf of Mexico outside my open window. Unable to sleep, I tossed and turned with almost the same regularity as the waves crashing on the beach. I was awake a long time, wondering if I seemed as lonely as she. Around three, I stumbled into the bathroom and threw up, a combination of alcohol and remorse. I slept a few hours before sunlight woke me. The sky was pale peach and pink with gray clouds bunched together like they had spent the night fighting. I tiptoed into the girls' room and woke Susan, telling her we needed to go home for church.

During the next two months, I was studying to finish my sociology degree and didn't call Ellen or hear from her. Susan continued her nightly telephone conversations with Rebecca, but only saw her at school and the end-of-the-year activities put on by elementary school parents. Each party was more lavish than the one preceding, the mothers and fathers in a war to surpass each other in their demonstrations of affection. I was hired to do research for the university's women's studies department and had to rely on our next-door neighbor to drive Susan to school functions. When Memorial Day came, she flew to California to spend the summer with her father, leaving me alone with my work.

In the empty house, I had time to think and felt guilty over the way I had let Ellen's and my friendship disintegrate. Although I wasn't responsible for her happiness, I didn't want to be accountable for her sadness. I called her with an invitation to meet at the coffee shop.

She arrived before I did and was sitting on the covered porch drinking iced coffee when I drove up. She had been reading a horse magazine, placed it on the table, and stood to shake my hand. I ordered coffee and brought my cup to her table. Her hair was longer and she looked younger. I wasn't sure if she had gained some needed weight or was rested. She told me she and her husband were spending a lot of time together.

"I think the beach house came between Jack and me. I was self-absorbed at that time. I'm sorry I wasn't a very good friend to you." A broad grin spreading over her face changed her into another person. I had never seen her smile before.

She said she had taken a hard look at her life and realized she didn't want to waste any more time. Jack's work in New Orleans had led to a job as lobbyist for the oil refining industry, and they were moving to Washington the end of July, so they would have time together before he started in September. They purchased an eighteenth century house on a hundred and fifty acre farm in Virginia. Sunlight was reflected in her pupils and her face glowed as she told me she was getting back into the horse business.

"I don't understand people," she said, "but I know horses. I've been up to see some Arabians and meet dealers in the region. I've got my eye on a black mare and Jack gave the owner a deposit. I plan to name her Miss Mobile."